**"What do you know about this setup?"
asked Durell.**

"Nothing," Jasmine said, in a way that told him she knew more.

Always before, Sam had taken McFee's orders without question. But this time, something wasn't right. "Do you think I may have to kill McFee?"

"Perhaps. Or the whole thing may be a trap, Sam. I think you have been selected as some kind of sacrificial lamb."

"Do you trust Colonel Chu?"

"No. Not at all."

"Good girl. Be suspicious. It's the only way to survive."

"Do you trust *me?*" she asked.

"No. Not a bit."

He slid into bed with her and held her long, firm body close to him. She tangled her long legs with his and made herself utterly fluid against him.

It had been a long time, from Singapore to Taipei, since he had been with a girl like this. He accepted her then, as she accepted him, lovers for the moment, but with a dark area of reserve, danger, and suspicion between them.

Assignment . . . .
PEKING

One

THE MAN IN THE MASK STRUGGLED IN THE DARK-
ness of his nonidentity.

Blinded, mute, held motionless more by self-imposed
discipline than by his orders, he floated in the black anti-
septic nowhere-nobody environment for a time beyond
his reckoning. There were long hours when he thought he
could not endure. There were days of passive emptiness
when he was a sieve, a sponge, alternately absorbing, re-
jecting, testing, weighing all that was poured into him.

Now he heard the voice, imperative and quiet, as insidious as a snake in the dark world he inhabited.

"Durell? Sam Durell?"

He lay silent and motionless in his black tomb of self-
denial.

"Durell, are you in there?"

*In where? Out here? Down in this place? Up in the
black spinning vault of space?*

"Sam, please answer me. It is quite all right. You can
answer. Vertical Five. It's important. Please, Sam."

He let the silence spin itself out after the sly, insidious
echoes. He was not here. He was not there. The name
meant nothing. There was no voice. No one called to
him.

He laughed and felt cunning. He thought, "It is said by
the ancient sages that a man must not shout unless he is
certain of an echo."

*Do not ask for help or love unless you are certain it
will be provided.*

Silence!

Then he heard a scratching sound, a faint clink of
metal on metal. There was quiet, sustained breathing.

The man's voice called again.

"Major Shan! Shan Tze Peng!"

"I am here," said Durell.

"Mr. Shan, I will get you out of here. I shall save you!"

The words were a lie, the friendship and anxiety a deceit. He smelled danger. He smelled death breathing outside the door. The clicking was too frantic, the effort to open the locked door was an effort not to save, but to kill. He could not know this for certain, but he felt it. His sense of danger made all his nerves tighten, made a muscle jump under the bandages on his cheeks, the pads over his eyes.

He sat up. He was not supposed to touch any of the bandages over his face, but his hands came up carefully, found the surgical tape under his ears and on his forehead, and he pulled them away with caution. He kept his eyes closed. He was afraid to open them. Then the fevered scratching at the door made him swing his legs off the edge of the bed and stand up. He had to see. It meant his life. Greentree would be furious, but it couldn't be helped. He opened his eyes.

Swimming mist. A glow of light. Then sharp focus. He was in a room softly illuminated by a globular lamp, furnished with a huge Chinese red-lacquered bed, some elegant chairs copied from the Tangs. There was a silky yellow carpet, carved teak cabinets with a collection of fine porcelain and jade. He looked about in wonder. There was one wide window, covered with a knotted net curtain embroidered with an elaborate border. He knew there were bars and screens over the window. Dominating one wall of the room was a vast lacquered screen, a painted copy of a Chinese antique of a thousand years ago. On the other side of the room was a mirror, full-length, framed in gilt, topped by two elaborately carved wooden dragons.

"Shan! Shan Tze Peng!" The voice outside was an urgent whisper. "Can you let me in? The lock is difficult."

He stared at the mirror, unmoving. His breath came slowly, regularly, but controlled with an immense effort. He saw his image as a tall man, a Chinese, with a round face, dark-skinned, a northern nose like that of a man from Shantung, with heavy black hair and dark brown eyes under the folded Oriental lids. There were little stainless steel clips still in place at his eyelids, and pale, fading scars on his round cheeks. He had a thin black moustache. His eyes smarted, and he blinked them and drew a deep breath and looked at the white shirt and tennis slacks and shoes he wore.

It was the first time in three weeks that he had seen himself.

"Greentree, you son of a bitch," he whispered.

"Shan?" the voice pleaded outside.

"Yes," he said.

"Help me, Major Shan."

"Yes."

"I will save you from these devils!"

"Yes," he said a third time.

He kept staring at his reflected image in the tall golden mirror. Then he shoved the face bandages that had masked him under the rumpled bedding of the big Chinese platform bed, and he went to the door.

He knew very well that the lock on the door was difficult. It had been devised by experts. It took two keys, and they had to be manipulated simultaneously, each in a different sequence of turns, more difficult than the average lock on a bank vault. He would be safe if he ignored the man trying to get in. But he couldn't be ignored. His sense of danger was more urgent by the moment.

He had no weapon, and for a moment he scanned the room, looking for something he could use—a scroll, a piece of wood, something to weight his hand. He could kill with any of these or, if necessary, with none of them. What was it the ancient fighting monks of China had said? Forbidden by their creed to use ax or knife, they left their monasteries and made every finger a dagger, each arm a spear, the open hand a sword. So was the art of judo born centuries ago. He flexed his fingers and swore silently again at Greentree.

"Major Shan! Please!" came the muffled voice.

"Coming," Durell said.

He lit a joss stick before a little jade image of Kuan Yin, the goddess of mercy, and went to the door.

He manipulated the inner locks carefully, aware of a sudden silence outside, a quiet waiting like the shadow of death in the night. He knew by what the intruder had said to him that his life was already forfeited. The man had made a mistake. But maybe it had been a deliberate test. In this business you never knew the full deviousness of an opponent's mind. It was better never to underestimate the enemy. Too many good men he had known were dead now in dark corners of the world because of a moment's hesitation, a dependence on a friend, an instant's lowering of caution's armor.

He opened the door.

A shadow leaped, a knife flickered like a serpent's tongue. Eyes glared, a contorted face closed on him, eyes suddenly wide with amazement and recognition, then fixed on the tiny steel clips that glittered on the eyelids, the fading hairline scars on the round cheeks of a face from Shantung. There was an explosion of breath, a moment of horror. The knife came up, ripping for the gut.

Night stars glittered outside over Sun Moon Lake. He glimpsed the cottages with their upturned eaves, tiled roofs, red-painted moon gates and low walls.

Then the edge of his palm clipped the wrist of the hand that held the knife thrusting for his belly. The blade was diverted, hissing through cloth. The attacker did not drop the knife. He was strong and sinuous, sliding to the right, and Durell jumped, struck, avoided a second upthrust, chopped again, missed. His opponent was professional, one of the best. In the dim light of the single globular lamp on the teak chest, he saw that the man, a Chinese, had a round Cantonese face and extraordinary shoulder development.

"Are you Shan?" the man whispered. They circled each other warily in the big room. "You look like him. Yes, exactly like him. But Shan is dead. The KMT caught him. But you are Shan, are you not?"

"Were you sent to kill me?" Durell asked.

"Not if you are really Shan."

"Of course you must kill me," Durell said. "I've been kept here for a month."

"Were you talking?"

"Of course I talked."

"I see."

"You see nothing," Durell said. "Who sent you?"

They circled once more, and again the knife flickered, snaking up and down and out, feinting. Durell moved in and the man stepped back toward the big lacquered screen against the wall opposite the bed. The man suddenly came at him and Durell jumped back, jumped up on the big platform bed, avoided the knife, and came down again toward the open door.

"You will die, Shan!"

"Not yet."

He swept up the lamp, yanking the cord loose, and threw it. It exploded with a small crash that broke the silence of their struggle. Darkness folded in. There was another crash as the Cantonese went into the lacquered screen. Sparks flew as the big tape recorders hidden there were torn loose. The sputtering was brief, sudden. The man's face looked detached, floating in the darkness. Durell came in low, felt a prick of the knife under his left arm; then his stiff fingers hit the man in the groin, came in again low in the belly, stabbed up for the face. There was a stifled scream, a wrenching away from him, a flicker of shadow at the door.

Durell ran after him. He could not afford to let the man get away.

The starlit night was cool. Wind soughed in the pines on the hillside overlooking Sun Moon Lake. Only a few dim lights showed in the other cottages scattered on the wooded mountainside. Stars reflected in the shimmering lake. It was long after midnight. Most of the houses were occupied by vacation people from Taipei, army men with their mistresses, a few American tourists to Taiwan, a discreetly managed brothel down the carefully tended path to the docks on the waterfront.

He did not spot his opponent. He stepped into the

black shadows of the upturned, tiled eaves. The breeze blew stronger for a moment, smelling of pines and charcoal smoke.

The Sun Moon Lake area, the most scenic of old Formosa, was only a seven-hour drive south from Taipei below the East-West Cross Island highway. The scents of autumn were in the air. Down the mountainside at the dock area were the simple hostels for tourists and the one modern hotel, the Evergreen, about a mile away. He could see the rowboats and launches that took sightseers by day to the Wen Wu temple, the aboriginal village of Tsung Shao, and the small islet in the center of the lake, called the "Gem of Formosa." Everything slept under the midnight stars. He had objected to this site during the three weeks that Greentree, McFee, and Colonel Chu Yi-fen had kept him in seclusion here, since it seemed to him like a place whose very isolation invited an easy breach of security. Now, when the training and work were almost over, the tapes ended, and Greentree's labors complete, it had happened.

Durell bit back his anger, and concentrated on searching the dark night, listening and watching.

The house where he had lived stood on a rocky outcropping among the mountain pines. A jeep trail led in a twisting route down toward the lake, far below. The wind felt cold. He shivered briefly. There were two smaller cottages here, like tiny jewels of Chinese temples. The jeep was parked before the one that Dr. Greentree shared with Colonel Chu. It was dark and silent over there. Durell considered the garden. An old stone lantern bulked between himself and the moon gate in the compound wall. There was an unaccustomed shadow under the stone lamp, and he moved with three long strides toward it and knelt beside the man who sprawled facedown on the carefully raked pebbles of the path.

It was one of Colonel Chu's men who ordinarily stood watch—a tough, slender old veteran of the Kuomintang's flight from mainland China to Taiwan. His grizzled head was bloody, and his mouth was open in death's inevitable surprise. What had killed him was a knife blow just under the heart. He had been knocked out first, so murder had been gratuitous, unnecessary. It told Durell something about the man who was hiding from him nearby.

He straightened silently. The soughing of the wind stopped and in the brief quiet he heard the faintest crunch of a shoe on the pebbled path beyond the moon gate. He waited for the pine-scented breeze again, then moved rapidly to the left of the gate. The wall was only five feet high. Low shrubs grew along it. With a fluid movement he put his hands on top of the wall and vaulted over it. He almost came down on the assassin crouching there.

"Shan, no!"

The man's words came with an explosive burst of breath. Durell glimpsed white, liquid eyes, and then his quarry was up and running, careless of noise, smashing through the pine trees. He had taken the path toward the lake.

Durell was only a few steps behind him.

For some moments he could see nothing but the slashing pine branches, and his opponent knew the way better than he. The distance between them lengthened. In a minute, the man was lost to sight in the dark woods.

Durell swung left, came out on the jeep track, and ran at top speed down its rutted path. The road was twisted, longer than the way through the pines but easier to cover. Now and then he glimpsed the lake. Across from the eastern shore were the bamboo rafts of the aborigines. During the day these semi-wild people performed a "Pestle Dance" for visiting tourists. He wondered if the assassin were headed that way.

He paused at the second switchback in the trail. The wind died again. The surface of the lake mirrored the stars. Two lights twinkled on the opposite shore, a lamp glowed in the island temple, a night light shone in one of the Evergreen Hotel windows. A bird called sleepily. Durell shivered again. With eyes adjusted to the starlight, he could see more details now. Stooping, he picked up a stone that fitted smoothly into his hand and clenched his fist over it.

Now he heard his quarry coming, jumping and sliding downhill toward him. A little to the right perhaps. Durell took a dozen steps and paused under a towering pine. The assassin was panicky, noisy in his haste to escape.

The man burst out of the wooded hillside only two steps away.

Instantly, Durell was under him, his body low, blocking the hurtling figure, tumbling the man head over heels into the road. The impact knocked Durell sidewise, off his feet, and he rolled over twice and came up to leap on his opponent's dark, sprawled figure. The man was good; he made a quick recovery. His fingers stabbed at the throat, missed, and his knee came up savagely; he grunted and wriggled aside. Durell caught one flailing arm and pinned him down and smashed at the face with the stone in his fist. The man's head thudded backward on the ground. Durell hit the contorted face once more and heard teeth and jawbone splinter.

The body under him went limp.

He did not release his grip. He rolled the man over, off the jeep road. The slanted eyes were open and blank, the face deceptively relaxed, except for the blood that oozed from his broken mouth. Breath whispered faintly from the parted, everted lips.

"Who are you?" Durell gasped.

There was no answer.

"Come on, you can speak. How did you find me?"

The breathing stopped.

"Tell me, or——"

There was a smell of cyanide on the last exhaled breath that escaped the assassin's lungs. A broken capsule gleamed between the shattered teeth.

The man was dead.

Two

TWO HOURS LATER, DURELL'S ANGER WAS UNA-bated.

"He knew me," he said. "He called me by name, by my real name, before he called me Major Shan."

"Take it easy," Greentree said.

"I can't take it easy. Everything is blown. The cover is gone."

"Not necessarily. Sit still."

"Ike, you've wasted all your time."

"Be still, will you?" Dr. Greentree was pedantic and patient. Durell could just see the surgeon's narrow, intellectual face beyond the glare of the surgical lights. The metal table on which he sat felt cold under his thighs. He looked beyond Ike Greentree's gold-rimmed World War II aviator's glasses. Somewhere in the background, outlined against the dawn that made the barred windows gray, was Colonel Chu's silent, elegant figure. Durell felt a twinge of pain in his eyelid as the last tiny steel clip was removed from his flesh. Greentree clicked his tongue with satisfaction and said, "Good. It's beautiful. Really beautiful, Sam. There won't be a mark left in three days."

"To hell with it," Durell said.

Colonel Chu spoke in his precise Oxonian accent. "I have sent the man's body to our intelligence people in Taipei. It should be there in an hour, old boy. Photographs, skin analysis, clothing—nothing much to tell us, there—and fingerprints and autopsy are scheduled. The files are open for it. We should have him identified before the day is over."

"And if you don't?" Durell asked angrily.

Colonel Chu shrugged.

Durell said: "So it's blown. I repeat it, they *know*. The whole damned gimmick is off. And I'm a dead man."

"Then so will I be," said Chu.

13

"You're damned easy about it," Durell sighed.

Chu laughed. "My inscrutable Oriental fatalism, you think? Let's switch to the Mandarin now, Cajun. You're Major Shan Tze Peng from this moment on. For three weeks, you are Major Shan in the flesh."

"A wonderful job," Ike Greentree said. He was engrossed in his professionalism. "It's a bit unusual, you see, reversing Occidental features to Chinese. In Hawaii, of course, some of my plastic surgeon colleagues have quite a practice making Oriental girls into Westerners. A simple operation, really. But with you, Sam, the problem was to make the job reversible, so we can turn you back into Sam Durell when your job is done."

"We'll never get off the ground," Durell said.

"Mandarin, please, Shan," Chu insisted gently.

"You can get up now," Greentree said. He stood back to let Durell off the surgical table. "Lovely job. Really lovely. You understand what I've done? The Oriental eyelid is a feature of the epicanthic fold, you see. I worked on the lateral canthus, where the eyelids join, to narrow and elevate its ap.earance. Western eyes have a redundancy of this fold. ut the Eastern 'slanted eye' does not have this extra lav of flesh to be eliminated. Rather than excise the fold mpletely—which could not then be returned to its orig al appearance—I've inverted the eyefold so we can r produce the upper lid the way it once was. Nothing t worry about. Really, nothing. To all intent and purr es, the upper lid fold *has* been eliminated and your e s are now—ah—Chinese. How do the contact lenses el?"

"The .ch," Durell said.

"M or Shan—Mandarin, yes?" Chu asked softly.

" t to Ike," Durell said. "Ike Greentree speaks Germa , Italian, Polish, Yiddish, and Cantonese. Mandarin i for gentlemen and Peking government bureaucrats."

Dr. Greentree smiled tightly. He was not amused. "Be careful of those lenses, Samuel. You would look odd, if you lost them, as a blue-eyed Chinese."

"All right, Ike."

"Everything is healed. Beautifully, lovely. By the time

Chu flies you into Red China, the surgical marks won't be found. Your skin, of course, was another problem. Your Cajun ancestry makes the texture and color impossible, of course. The pigmentation pills you've been taking are derived from trioxsalen, which sensitizes and mobilizes the melanin cells of the dermis to react to the stimulation of ultraviolet light. That's why you've been under the lamps daily. Washington thought this method safer than trusting to theatrical makeup dyes to get your skin this brownish-yellow color. It's from the inside out, so to speak. Much safer, yes. Your skin color will certainly last for the three weeks you will be in the People's Republic of China with Colonel Chu."

"Chu isn't staying with me," Durell said. "He just flies the airplane."

Colonel Chu smiled and lit a cigarette. Ike Greentree picked up a large glossy photograph from his desk and studied it, comparing it with swift glances at Durell. Durell knew it was a dossier enlargement of a man once known as Shan Tze Peng, an agent of L-5's Taiwan Department in Peking. The man in the photo had been quietly killed in Taipei, over a month ago, to allow Durell to take his place.

"Fortunately," said Greentree, "your hair is black and naturally straight, Sam. But your Caucasian facial bone structure was a hell of a job. The idea was to make your face as round and Chinese as the original Shan's. We could have injected silicone directly, as in the illegal, cosmetic breast surgeries sometimes performed for entertainers——"

Chu laughed. Durell said, "Thanks for nothing."

"——but that would have been dangerous. The fluid sometimes sags and moves about in the body tissues. Not to mention all sorts of dangerous side effects, speaking physiologically. So I worked on your malar prominences —those cheek scars you have are invisible now—and I inserted a plastic bag of the proper shape in each cheek, preformed to round your face to the contours of Shan's, lodging the plastic in the subcutaneous tissue. They're filled with a thin, oily silicone fluid, so your flesh is quite soft and malleable. Very natural to the touch and normal in its action when you talk or eat. The preshaped bag keep the fluid from moving away from where it's been implanted. The plastic is tough enough so you needn't worry about its failing as a prosthetic device. And to reverse what I've done, surgically, will be a simple matter of removing the plastic shapes when you get back."

"*If* I get back," Durell said, looking at the elegant Colonel Chu.

Ike Greentree frowned. "You're the field agent, Sam. I've seen your file. You've come through a lot in the past."

"My survival factor is down to 0.56," said Durell.

"Well . . ."

"And I ought to retire."

Chu drawled, "Does anyone ever retire from our business, Mr. Shan?" He was impatient, watching the dawn brighten beyond the cottage windows. "Are you quite finished with him, Dr. Greentree?"

ke sighed, then nodded decisively. "Yes. I've done all I an. Add my work to Durell's ninety-seven percent re- ll capacity from those tapes, and his mnemonic abilities om other training sources, and—yes, he is now Shan fze Peng."

"All right, then. Good," the Chinese said. Chu wore his Nationalist China military uniform with easy authority. He fixed Durell with dark, opaque eyes. "From now on, Shan, nothing but Mandarin. Your life depends on it."

Three

IT WAS A SEVEN-HOUR DRIVE NORTH TO TAIPEI, AND when they had done three hours of it and stopped at Taichung to eat, Durell was thoroughly tired of listening to Colonel Chu's exquisite Mandarin.

"We should have arranged your training and the surgery in Tainan, far south," the KMT man said. "So few people go there, although it is a lovely old town. Have you ever seen the rebel Koxinga's temple there? And giant old banyan trees. I wonder if your assassin had been hiding out in Tsung Shao, with the aborigines? We must clean those people out of there, one day—but they do bring in tourist dollars. It will be difficult to arrange."

In Taichung there were water buffalo, rice paddies like geometric lakes, and laundry floating from long bamboo poles, and, higher up, farmers picking tea on the hillside. It was warmer here, down from the elevation of the lake. There were many Nationalist Army trucks on the roads.

"You do not say much, Shan," Chu complained.

"You talk enough for both of us."

"Come, we must be friends. We are in this dangerous matter together, are we not?"

"All you do is fly the plane in and out. I'm the fellow who jumps. And I still don't know why."

"You will be completely briefed this evening. Then all will be clear to you."

"I'll bet."

"You are—how do you say it?—a most reluctant dragon, sir. Quite different from what I had heard of you."

"Because I have sense enough to be afraid?"

"Fear is healthy, sir. It sharpens the wits. But one must have the moral purpose to pursue one's course despite danger."

Durell didn't bother to answer. He liked the purposeful control of Colonel Chu less and less. A month ago he had been on rest leave back home in the bayous, at Peche Rouge, deep in the Louisiana delta country. It had been good to spend those quiet days with the old gentleman, his grandfather Jonathan. He had been in Key West and Singapore before that, with four rich young ladies and Jasmine Jones, a Chinese prostitute from San Francisco. After that, the sounds of birds and water fowl along the dark green canals and narrow chênières of the delta country were like a restful symphony. He was, and had been for some years, an assistant chief in charge of field operations for K Section, that anonymous, trouble-shooting branch of the Central Intelligence Agency, under General Dickinson McFee, who answered only to Joint Chiefs and a weekly briefing in the President's private sitting room at the White House.

Durell often told himself he had been in the business too long, but it was the only life he had known ever since early OSS and G2 days, following his law degree at Yale. It was all a long time ago, he reflected grimly when he considered the gray in his black hair, the furrow of lines around his eyes and mouth, the look he had acquired that marked him, despite the easy litheness with which he mo. ᵈ as a man set apart from other men. He was big, with a heavy musculature; but he had the slender, facile fingers of a gambler, and he was as deft at cards as old Grandpa Jonathan, who had been among the last of the old-time Mississippi riverboat gamblers.

The hulk of the *Tr is Belles,* once one of the most graceful of river sidewh ᵉlers, was now the one place Durell counted as home, s᷍ ᵉne in her mudbank in the soft green light of the bayou He had spent part of his leave sleeping or drifting abou₁ ʰe old galleries and decks, the faded, dusty salons and b ˡroom, or talking gently to the old man up in the pilot hᴸ ᵗse above the hurricane deck. It had been a calm, quiet veek, but he knew he could never stay there in spirit. T time for changing his habits of life was long past. There vere red-tabbed dossiers on him in Moscow's priority fil in the grim offices of the Soviet KGB; and more, sinc the Singapore assignment and Jasmine Jones, in L-5 up t Peking. He was marked as extremely dangerous. He knew intimately most of the dark alleys of the world's cities and a number of the shadowed corners of its jungles. He could kill, and had done so when needed, with a pencil, a rolled newspaper, a needle, or simply with the strong fingers of his graceful hands. He had seen friends die, too, in this shadow war of espionage and counterespionage, in a world too often and secretly threatened by atomic oblivion.

Now a new dimension had been added to his identity, and as Chu drove on and talked about the glorious aims

of the Generalissimo and the ambitions of the Kuomintang to return one day to mainland China, Durell rubbed
the side of his face softly, feeling roundness where there
had been bone and lean flesh, sensing the Oriental shape
of his eyes, the color of the skin on the back of his hands.
He felt a duality not easy to adopt or accept. He was Sam
Durell of K Section, and he was Major Shan Tze Peng of
Peking's dreaded L-5—all at once, in a personality iden-
tification that would be difficult to control.

"You are perfect," Colonel Chu said softly. "When I
spotted and arranged to kill the original Major Shan in
Taipei, it was all done with the utmost discretion. An op-
portunity of a lifetime, thanks to the skills of Dr. Greentree. No one ever heard a whisper of Shan's death."

"Don't congratulate yourself," Durell said. "Somebody
heard of it."

"How is that?"

"Otherwise, why did a killer come for me?"

They left Taichung, with its National Museum housing
China's treasures of calligraphy, bronzes, porcelains, and
jade from the old Imperial treasure house, and by midaf-
ternoon were on the outskirts of Taipei, the island capital.
Here and there they had passed small settlements of nuns
and monks growing tea and vegetables to trade for rice.
At Pital, the Green Lake seven miles south of the city,
Chu halted again for tea, and they sat briefly on a small
terrace overlooking the town of Hsintien. Far below, the
massive rock cliffs kept the lake in perpetual, mysterious
shadows. Boatmen crossed its surface like Venetian gon-
doliers, gliding under the delicate suspension bridge that
swayed above the glistening Hsintien River.

The scream of a jetliner lowering for Taipei International Airport accompanied them into the Nationalist
capital. The tranquillity of small villages, paddy lands,
and terraced mountainsides was abruptly shattered by the
noise and stinks of the streets. Chu guided the car expertly through the hubbub of the downtown district along
Heng Yang Road and Westgate, turned north past the
China House on Chung Shan, which was crowded with

tourists eager for coral jewelry, straw-plaited goods, Tientsin-style rugs, buffalo-horn souvenirs. Chu seemed to be taking a devious route.

"Are we being followed?" Durell asked quietly.

"It is always possible, is it not?"

"Not only possible. Probable."

"But the work done on you was perfect! With uttermost security, Shan. And yet——"

"Yet someone found me back there."

Chu nodded. "So I take precautions. Be patient."

They twisted and turned through Taipei's streets and alleys. All of Durell's training and instinct were turned to spot anyone on their trail. Taipei was a relatively new city, named by the old Manchu government a hundred years ago. Its old walls and huge gates reflected some of the old Empire charm, but the buildings were generally ugly, with few temples except for the bright coloration of the Lungshan Buddhist temple in the Wan Hua district, one of the original areas of the city. Its stone sculpture and the delicate wood carvings on its ornate roof slid by the windows of Chu's car. Durell could not detect anyone following them, but Chu was not satisfied.

At the hub of the city, near New Park and the southern gate, they passed the chief executive government buildings, not far from the bust of General Chennault of the Flying Tigers.

"There," Chu said. "One of *them*."

He lifted a delicate finger to indicate a middle-aged man admiring the Mei Ling orchids in the government park, under tall and graceful palm trees. The man raised his head, as if he could hear them in the car as they passed, but his glance seemed casual enough.

"From Peking?" Durell asked.

"Of course."

"Why is he free to roam about, then?"

"It is better to learn from him than to kill him."

"Then you should have kept Major Shan alive, so I could live with him for a bit, and learn some of his mannerisms," Durell pointed out. "And it's five o'clock. Do I get briefed sometime this year?"

"He has not followed us," Chu said, making a display of considering his rear-vision mirror. "We go there now."

They crossed the Chungshan bridge, passed the zoo and the Martyr's Shrine on a small hillside, skirted the Shilin Institute of Horticulture and halted at the Ma Tsu Hotel, named after the ancient goddess of the sea. It was near the site of what had originally been a Japanese Shinto shrine, remodeled into a spectacular example of Chinese palace-style architecture. Built on the hill north of the city and the Tanshui River, it overlooked the sprawling capital and was less than ten minutes from the downtown shopping area.

Chu stopped the car some distance from the main gate entrance to the Ma Tsu. "It would not be discreet," he murmured, "to be seen together from this point on. Your room is number 404 in the Green Dragon section. You can find it by walking around the pool behind the lobby. The dragon is in the center of the pool. Your briefing officer will be waiting. You will see me tomorrow. We fly to the mainland then."

They shook hands. Chu's fingers were soft and smooth and cool. The Chinese smiled. "I wish you had more enthusiasm for this project, Mr. Shan."

"I might, when I know what it is," Durell said.

He got out and walked in the late afternoon sunlight through the gate and up the ornate drive between lush shrubbery to the main lobby. The lobby, done in Manchu Imperial style, had ornate green columns, a carp pool, a rock garden, and a fretted, timbered ceiling that let in the evening light. It was more crowded with American and Nationalist military uniforms than with civilian tourists. There was a bar called the Three Golden Coins to his left as he entered, and jazz music came from there. Under palms and reproductions of giant Ming vases were settees and lounges in cloistered groups ensuring privacy. A wall of glass shimmered with an emerald fish tank, in which brilliant tropical creatures darted and flashed. It was the cocktail hour, and it seemed to Durell that he had been away from civilization for much longer than the three weeks of isolated surgery and training with Ike Greentree and Colonel Chu.

He paused just inside the elegant doors, aware of seeing something or someone familiar out of the corner of his eye. He didn't turn his head immediately for a better look. Assuming a manner that Major Shan would have used, he walked to the desk. The Chinese clerk regarded him blandly, indifferently, and he suddenly realized he was being greeted as a Chinese himself, rather than as an American. It made a difference.

"The key to 404, please," he said in Mandarin.

"Sir?" The clerk replied in English.

"Major Shan's key, please."

"Oh, yes, sir. Of course. You are expected."

The key hung on a solid bronze replica of Ma Tzu, the sea goddess. There was a sense of wetness on the metal figurine, as if a sweaty hand had just relinquished it. He stared at the clerk.

"You are certain I am expected?"

"Yes, sir. Your reservation for tonight has been most highly honored."

Durell put the key in his left hand and turned to survey the broad expanse of the lobby, looking again for the familiar note that had caught him among the people passing in and out. Nothing. American generals, aiguilletted aides, women tourists overloud in describing their day's bargains, some young Chinese women.

Then he recognized Jasmine Jones.

Singapore. Madame Hung and her Seven Isles of Pleasure. Remembered pain, torture. And a friendly Chinese-American voice. A warm and urgent body. And then the tiny grill of steel pins skewering her lips together as punishment for talking to him, for offering him aid and comfort.

The images flickered through his mind and ended. Jasmine stood taller than most Chinese girls, long-legged and high-waisted, with firm arched breasts and strong thighs that the white silk frock made no attempt to conceal. She looked at him and through him and away, then touched a white-gloved little finger to her right cheek. Her Chinese face was thinner than most, and she had large, luminous black eyes under fine, arched brows. Durell thought he saw shock and disbelief in those eyes for the moment that her glance brushed across his. His own face showed nothing at all. He had recommended Jasmine for work with K Section after her help to him in Singapore the year before, but he hadn't followed through on it and had not known whether General McFee had accepted her.

Apparently he had.

Her signal with her finger to her cheek meant, *Be careful. I will follow you.*

He flipped his room key in his hand and walked out through the back of the lobby and around the wide pool, with its green stone dragon. His room was in a modern wing of box-crate architecture that could be found anywhere that tourists traveled in groups around the world. There were noisy tennis players on the courts nearby. Pretty Chinese serving maids in black skirts just a bit too short hurried back and forth with trays of drinks and food for the people at the pool. It was a bit too public, Durell thought. His room was on the second floor with a small private balcony overlooking the green dragon in the pool. An American girl in a pink bikini had climbed up on the stone dragon and was posing for her picture. Durell turned his key in the lock and pushed the door open with his fingertips.

Nothing happened.

Nobody shot at him. The room did not explode. The air inside, coolly air-conditioned, was scented with some spicy odor he found unattractive. He went in, using all the routine precautions against surprise, and did not think the effort wasted when Number 404 turned out to be just another impersonal, sterile hotel room.

He closed the door, but did not lock it, and checked the lamps and switches for listening devices, knowing how anxious the Generalissimo's intelligence organs were to get informal American opinions of themselves. He hadn't quite finished when he heard the door open and close quietly behind him. She hadn't wasted any time.

"It's all right," she said huskily. "The room is clean."

He turned and walked toward her and took her chin in his cupped hand, not saying anything, and almost brutally turned her face to the light from the window. He studied her mouth. A muscle twitched in her smoothly powdered cheek. Her lips quivered. On the upper lip and below the mouth were a number of tiny white pinpoint scars that nothing could erase.

"Do you doubt that I'm Jasmine?" she asked, her voice almost inaudible.

He let go of his grip on her face and spoke in Mandarin again. "I know. Who sent you?"

She spoke unnaturally, in English. "I can only speak California Cantonese, if you want to call it that. Isn't that ridiculous? I'm Chinese and can't speak my own language; and you're Sam Durell, dearest Sam, and I used to think I loved you. But now you look like one of my own people, and not at all like yourself, and I'm all mixed up and wish I'd never let McFee send me here. But he thought it best."

There were tears in her eyes.

He spoke in English. "Don't cry, Jasmine."

"You looked at my mouth. It's so ugly. All those little scars——"

He kissed her gently, deliberately. Her lips were cold under his. "Your mouth is beautiful."

"You can still see . . . what was done to me——"

"We all have scars, Jasmine."

She was shaking and looking at him with tortured bewilderment. "Oh, I think I'm going out of my mind! You sound like Sam, you touch me like Sam, but you look so —you're not——"

"I look like Major Shan Tze Peng."

"Yes."

"Are you the one who is to brief me?"

"No. General Haystead will do that."

"That son of a bitch?"

"He is in command of the operation."

"Over McFee? Over K Section?"

"McFee sent me to get you. He's here in Taipei. He

wants a private talk with you, because you've been loaned to the E Branch of the NSA."

"And the KMT." He was angry again.

"I wish——"

He waited, watching her.

"McFee is upset about you," she said.

"Why?"

"I don't know. And Deirdre Padgett is here with him and she doesn't hide very much. She hates me."

"Why do you think so?"

"She's your real girl, isn't she?"

He hesitated. "We've had a difference of opinion on the definition of love."

"Well, she does hate me, because . . . because I'm flying into China with you. As your wife."

He said, still trying to see behind her eyes, "Major Shan was not married. His wife in mainland China died."

"Yes, but that's all been arranged. Papers were filed everywhere, properly dated. L-5 in Peking was notified a week ago. Shan married a local Taipei girl." She smiled without meaning. "That's me. It was done because I'm supposed to help you in Peking. You will need a woman there, and McFee thought I should be the one."

He began to smile. "And Deirdre doesn't like this arrangement?"

"Hardly," Jasmine said.

"Let's go see them—McFee and Deirdre."

"Yes. In a minute."

He paused. "What is it?"

She was near tears. "Don't you think my mouth is ugly? The scars——"

"I can't see them now, Jasmine."

And he kissed her again.

Four

THEY WENT OUT IN SILENCE. HE DID NOT QUESTION her further. It was plain that the shock of seeing him transformed into a Chinese, into Shan Tze Peng, had thrown her off balance. He was aware of the quick, side-long looks she gave him as they walked toward the car park beside the hotel. Jasmine did the driving. She talked then, about Washington, and how McFee had hired her as an analyst at No. 20 Annapolis Street, K Section's headquarters, and how she had spent some weeks at the Maryland "Farm" where K section people were trained in their specialties. She was proud of her record there. She spoke too quickly, telling about it in a high, unnatural voice that betrayed her excitement.

The thought touched his mind that he should not and could not trust her. She had worked for Madame Hung's L-5 apparatus in Singapore; she was Chinese, and her po-litical loyalties could be anything. True, K Section's psy-chiatric tests were not easily fooled. But this girl had ex-traordinary intelligence, a quick perception, a gift for landing on her feet. Born in San Francisco, she could still be loyal to Peking.

Seated close beside her in the Humber she drove, he sensed her perfume, the womanly essence of her. He thought she was more than just desirable. He thought he would enjoy going into mainland China with her.

The streets were crowded, but she drove through them expertly. The sun had set, and the sky held a bright lime-green color in the west. Lamps twinkled; gaudy neon signs in Chinese characters flashed on and off. The smells of cooking were everywhere. In the old section of the city she parked in an alley, fumbled in her white purse for a cigarette, and Durell lit it for her with a brass Mexican lighter. Her mouth still trembled.

"We walk a bit," she said.

"McFree doesn't like slums," Durell commented, looking at the poverty about them. "He's a fastidious little man."

"But he and Deirdre are not supposed to be here. It's all unofficial. General Haystead made that plain."

"Better and better," Durell said glumly.

They walked out of the alley into the evening throngs on the streets. Jasmine was almost as tall as he. Her heels made steady clicking sounds as she moved her long legs. "I can't get over it," she said. "It's as if you are hidden somewhere under that Chinese face, Sam."

"I certainly hope so."

"But it's disturbing to me. Last year, in Singapore——"

"That was another time and place, Jasmine. ⟨...⟩ I wouldn't be alive today if it weren't for you."

"You don't owe me anything," she murmured.

They didn't have far to go. They turned up another alley and came to a brick wall with a red-painted wooden gate. Durell looked back at the street, but still could not spot anyone following them. Jasmine pulled on an iron chain, and somewhere beyond the gate a deep gong sounded. There was a click, and the way was opened for them. Inside was a formal garden, with stone lanterns shedding a soft yellow light on a trickling brook, circular stepping-stones, a glimmering house with squat columns and a broad flight of steps. It was, or had been, an old temple. Durell followed the tall girl into this other world, abruptly remote from the noise of the streets and alleys. He was not surprised by this place. Dickinson McFee was an unpredictable man.

A white-coated Cantonese bowed and smiled in the elaborate doorway. "Welcome, Mr. Shan. Welcome, Miss Jasmine Jones. This way, please."

Jasmine hung back. "You go alone. I think Deirdre would rather I weren't around."

Durell followed the servant into a room in the back of the converted temple. There was a delicate scent in the air, a feeling of detachment from all the world. He remembered clearly when he had last seen Deirdre Padgett,

and for a moment her image moved in him with remembered pain, despite all his efforts at indifference. They
had been in love for many years, although he had often
told her that it was too dangerous in his business to allow
himself to grow vulnerable emotionally. He felt the
enemy could always strike at him through her, through
his love for her. And although they had discussed marriage, he had always withdrawn from that final step. He
did not want her exposed to hurt or danger, either for
herself or because of what might always happen to him.
His own life, he thought, had long ago been forfeited to
the enemy.

Deirdre had met his objections with unswerving, total
devotion. And then, against his wishes, she had joined K
Section, first as a Control Resident in Rome, and then as
General Dickinson McFee's personal aide and secretary.

It was more than a year since they had seen each other
now.

He felt her presence in the room before he actually saw
her. It had always been like that between them. He felt
an inner shock that somehow he was able to control, and
the words he wanted to speak were effectively checked.
He turned to her with his new face bland and calm.

"Hello, Dee."

She stood very still, then whispered, "You are Major
Shan."

"You know me, Deirdre."

"Yes, of course."

She was not as tall as Jasmine, and her raven hair was
immaculately done in a coronet and French knot. Her
eyes, luminous and brilliant, regarded him with the same
element of shock that Jasmine had exhibited. But something was missing. She did not smile. She did not walk
closer to him. Her body, which he had come to know so
intimately, was very still and remote. She wore a gold
Pucci sheath that enhanced every fine line and curve of
her figure.

He smiled faintly. "Am I such a stranger, then, Deirdre? I know how I look, but——"

"It's not that."

"What is it, then? Jasmine thinks——"

"Jasmine? No. Yes. A little. But you have your orders."

"Jasmine is a fine girl," he said.

"Yes."

"But there's something else."

"You and General Haystead—McFee is concerned."

"About what?"

"He'll tell you. This way."

They hadn't touched or kissed or expressed intimacy in any way. He kept his face blank as she turned and led him through other rooms of the silent, elegant house. Through a back door she walked into a garden, and on a bench ~~~~~ ~~~~~ ~~~~ed by tall oleanders and hibiscus, he saw Genral McFee.

The chief of K Section, who was as much a mystery to Durell after all these years as he was to most of the intelligence world, looked small and gray and relatively innocuous, with his knobby blackthorn stick upright between his knees. Durell knew that lethal stick, with the poisoned dart at its tip and the explosives and knives built into it by the gadget boys in K Section's lab. He had been threatened by it once, and he never knew, even today, if McFee had been bluffing. It sometimes seemed to him that McFee was the one man he'd ever met who had no soul or conscience.

The gray eyes in the gray face of the gray man regarded him without depth or meaning, and when McFee spoke Mandarin it was with superb elegance. "Mr. Shan, of course. And you are surprised to see me in Taipei?"

"Pleasantly surprised, sir."

"I do travel occasionally, Mr. Shan, when the situation is grave enough to warrant it."

Durell waited. Brilliantly colored birds in bamboo cages hung about the garden sang their evening songs. He watched Deirdre move almost protectively to a position behind McFee. Her eyes, too, were blank and hostile.

"Is something wrong, sir?" he asked quietly. "I didn't ask for this assignment, you remember. I don't like having to change the way I am. There are a lot of things about this affair that I don't trust or understand——"

"Exactly."

"And you don't trust me, General?"

"No. I do not."

"To do the job satisfactorily?"

"It is a situation," McFee said precisely, "that has placed you, myself, and perhaps the world in the gravest danger. You are under Haystead's orders. Nothing I could do back in Washington could countermand that." McFee almost smiled. Not quite. "Even *I* am neither omniscient nor omnipotent, whatever the image I may project."

"I still don't understand."

"It's quite simple. I had you brought here for only a few brief words and they are this. In the course of your projected work ahead, you may find that you and I are in total disagreement as to procedure. You will have to make a grave decision. I shall not influence you one way or another. I can give you no orders." McFee paused and looked at him with eyes as cold as Antarctic ice.

Durell remained silent.

"Have you ever heard of the Six Sentinels?"

"No, sir."

"You are sure?"

"Yes, sir, I am sure. As for doubting my loyalty to you——"

"I know your loyalties, Cajun." McFee's voice changed very subtly. "You pretend to be indifferent to all but the job at hand. It's your profession. Under its rules, you know the risks you have taken, the dangers you have welcomed, to do what you felt was in accord with your principles. You are a Puritan, Samuel, and a patriot. You ask for no bugles or medals for the work you do, and you pretend to scorn them. You would be the first to deny your dedication to the free world. And perhaps," McFee sighed, "all this is a fault."

Durell looked at Deirdre. Still remote, she seemed to him the loveliest and most desirable woman in the world; and he had met and known many marvelous women. He was touched by anger, shock, and a lack of comprehension. He came to no decisions. He felt the unfamiliar contours of his strange face and wondered how deep the change in him had really been effected.

"Who are the Six Sentinels, sir? I don't even know yet what my job is to be. Chu flies me to China tomorrow. Now I understand that Jasmine goes with me. What am I to do or accomplish in Peking?"

McFee waved a hand in dismissal. "Haystead will tell you all that."

For one of the rare times in his life, Durell felt utterly at a loss. He felt betrayed by the hostility emanating from Deirdre and McFee. It didn't make sense. He had done nothing but obey orders, blindly and reluctantly, in this instance. His instincts, he reflected numbly, had been right after all. There was something in this particular job that went far beyond anything he had been ordered to do in the past. A sense of enormous darkness and danger touched his mind. He looked at Deirdre, but she stood silently, impassive, lovely and cool and distant, behind McFee.

"I know you won't tell me more," he said quietly, "for reasons of your own. I can only promise that I'll do what I think is best. I want help from you, some direction, but it's obviously not forthcoming."

"We cannot help you, Sam. We don't know enough ourselves to advise you on what may come of this affair." McFee stood up. He kept his lethal blackthorn stick ready in his hand. "All I can do is warn you that nothing in the coming weeks will be what it appears. In a way, I'm depending on you to learn, without the prejudice of absorbing my own opinions as to what is going on, the truth of certain suspicious dangers that have come to my attention without the slightest hard core of verification. And that is all."

He was being dismissed. "When do I see General Haystead?"

"Now. Jasmine will take you there."

"And what am I to report to him?"

"You are under Haystead's orders now," said McFee.

His eyes were like gray stones as he looked at Durell. And then he turned away. For a moment Durell thought that Deirdre hesitated. But then she left without looking back at him.

Five

GENERAL HARRY HAYSTEAD WAS ONE OF THOSE brilliant young Air Force generals considered a maverick by the majority of his fellow officers, too outspoken to be regarded with ease by the Washington establishment, and yet possessed of a dynamic drive and private influence that made him seem untouchable.

Jasmine drove Durell down into the center of the shopping district, among restaurants featuring Peking duck and Cantonese cooking, past food stalls where vendors sold dumplings and noodles, and then into a quiet street of American business branch offices. Most were already closed and dark for the day, but before I.P.S. Electronics she parked and sat still for a moment.

"I gather McFee really disturbed you, Sam."

"Yes, he did."

"And Deirdre?"

"I don't know what to make of it. I feel as if I'm being used, but I don't know how or why."

"Deirdre loves you, Sam. Desperately."

He said flatly, "I doubt that. Let's go."

General Haystead was waiting behind a broad, immaculate steel desk in a back office of the modern building. Durell knew that I.P.S. was a front for the National Security Agency's electronic warfare branch for espionage equipment. Most of the spy ships of the Navy were equipped with NSA gadgets and were virtually under the command of that agency's people. Electronic gadgetry could perform miracles in gathering, collating, synthesizing and analyzing an enormous multitude of data on enemy and friendly nations' industrial, economic, and military capacities. In a sense, the two or three power spheres of the world and their allies now enjoyed electronic and counterelectronic battles that the people of the world did not even dream about.

Haystead snapped an immaculate cuff back, looked at a complicated wristwatch, and said, "Five minutes late. Not too bad, considering you have a reputation for individualistic behavior. You will have to remedy that trait on this job, Durell."

"My name is Major Shan, sir," Durell said.

"Yes, yes. But we're safe here. No bugs, and nothing outside to pinpoint this room and pick up what we say. We're completely shielded, I guarantee it. Sit down."

Durell remained standing, his eyes giving nothing away to the uniformed man. Jasmine stood by the door. For Haystead, she did not exist. But then, nothing mattered to the general but his passion for the immediate job at hand. Everything about him betrayed a dynamic intensity that could be contagious to anyone but Durell. No one could doubt Haystead's patriotism, if the draped flags behind his desk and the massed ribbons on his chest meant anything. Durell had read enough of the man's published speeches to patriotic organizations and corporate conventions to know that with Haystead his country and its safety came first, guiding everything he did.

Haystead was one of the younger generation of generals whose work was practically autonomous, dealing as he did with highly classified electronic espionage. He moved briskly, cleanly, and Durell noticed his strong, immaculately scrubbed, stubby hands as he took dossier files from a desk drawer and neatly squared them on his blotter. Haystead had a round, clipped head of prematurely gray, grizzled hair, a flat face that was hard and uncompromising, and pale gray eyes that were almost too intense. About forty, he looked ten years younger. He gave the impression of limitless energy as he jerked his chin up and stared at Durell.

"I asked you to sit down," he snapped.

"I prefer to stand, General Haystead."

"I am not accustomed——"

"And I am not under military orders, sir."

"Yes. Too bad. Well . . ." His eyes, if possible, grew colder. "What do you know about the Nationalist general, Chien Y-Wu?" he snapped.

Durell's memory was triggered by the name. "General Chien went on an unauthorized flight over the mainland and was shot down, lost, or killed. Or defected. I saw a memo in my department to that effect about two months ago."

"Last July 21, to be exact. The flight was *not* unauthorized. Chien worked for us. By that I mean he had a position with the KMT here, of course, but he was under my order:, and I'm the man who sent him into China."

" see," Durell said.

Do you? A man has to admit mistakes, Durell—or Shan, or however you think of yourself now. I made a mistake with General Chien. But he was a genius, you 'now. He was great with our electronic data-gathering equipment. He knew enough——"

"I see," Durell said. "And Peking has him now. He isn't dead."

"Right."

"A prisoner?"

"We have reason to believe that his stay in Peking is not an unwilling one. We think he's been shooting his mouth off, to put it plainly. A big loose lip that can cost us plenty." Haystead's voice grated bitterly. "He's living in high style in a top-security Peking house with L-5 men all around him. We can't get a man near him. We've lost two so far just trying."

"So I'm the third that you're sending?"

"Yes."

"And you want me to find out if he's a traitor, a prisoner, or what?"

"We want you," Haystead said flatly, "to get him out of there. Bring him back, if you can. It's imperative that I talk with him. Urgent, you understand? He knows something that I must know. But if you can't get him out, kill him."

Durell nodded. It was not an unexpected assignment.

But there was more to it, he knew. He stood quietly, waiting, while Haystead's square, pale fingers adjusted the dossiers on his desk.

"You don't want the job?" Haystead asked finally.

"I didn't say that."

"You have a talent for saying a lot by saying precisely nothing."

"I want the rest of it," Durell said. "Two men have been killed, you say, trying to get to Chien. I'm the third. I don't want to strike out just because I don't know which direction the ball is coming from."

"Are you afraid?"

"I'm always afraid," Durell said quietly.

"Listen to me, Durell," Haystead rasped. "You've been most highly recommended. They say you're the best, the best available. If you fail, we're all in trouble. Big trouble."

"General Chien is just one man."

"Right. But there are people, powerful people, behind him. Do you understand what happens if Chien Y-Wu, who may well be an egomaniac, talks his head off and blows all our electronic data to L-5? The Peking regime is just aching for an outside diversion aimed directly against us. Things are getting chaotic in there, with resistance to Mao's Cultural Revolution. The old-liners who go back to Mao's Long March will jump at the chance to yell provocation—with proof—and wind up a few atomic toys for Taiwan. Ostensibly, their enemy would be the Kuomintang here. But we're committed to retaliate. A lot of our boys are just aching for *that* excuse, too." Haystead rubbed his forehead, the first human gesture of distress that Durell had observed. "Goddamit, it's a conspiracy on both sides, and that stupid Chien can trigger it into an atomic war."

"Do the Chinese Reds have the missiles and the atomic capabilities to start something?"

"Yes, they do. And there's a clique over there just hungry for it."

"And a group in Washington equally anxious to have

an excuse to answer?" Durell said. "I want to be clear on it."

"Now you're getting the real picture," Haystead snapped. "So what we don't know is who is going to try to stab you in the back before you get to Chien and shut Chien's mouth, understand? It could come from either side, as I said. The other two men we sent were good—damned good. But they were betrayed. There are traitors everywhere in this crazy world, Durell. People have lost their sense of perspective and have gone overboard on stupid ideologies and do-gooder schemes. Hell, *people* haven't changed for thousands of years. So the way I see it, it's short-sighted and dangerous."

Haystead paused. "Our people have forgotten the good old-fashioned virtues that have made this nation the greatest and strongest power in human history. Forget your disciplines and morality and you go under; you sink and die. Look at Rome, Athens. But what America has is worth fighting for, by God, and by all the good principles that made our nation great, I intend to fight for the right as long as I draw a breath in my body. All this soft-headed, socialist thinking in our courts and Congress can only lead to our own self-destruction. Traitors, yes, and they'll be after you to stop you, Durell. I can tell you, as you stand there right now, that at this moment your life isn't worth a plugged nickel."

As Haystead spoke, his words created a subtle metamorphosis in his face and figure. His body seemed to grow rigid with anger, and there was almost a Messianic look in his eyes that made Durell keep carefully silent. Then the man seemed to shiver and relax a little, and Durell said, "Just where are the traitors on our side, sir? In the Pentagon, perhaps?"

"I don't know," Haystead grumbled.

"In your own Air Force? You talk as if——"

Haystead flushed with new anger. "It could well be right in your own establishment, Durell. So watch yourself every step of the way. Trust no one. Your orders can come only from me, understand? No matter who speaks to you, or how long you may have known a man—or woman," he added, glancing for the first time at Jasmine, "you remember you belong just to me on this mission."

The general suddenly flipped the small folders on his desk toward Durell. He seemed very tired, all at once, and smiled with a startling, boyish shyness that was abrupt enough to seem genuine. "It's all there. The whole outline. Briefings on the people who will help you on the mainland. Read them, memorize them, and destroy them before you get on the plane with Chu. I understand you have top rating in mnemonic exercises."

For a second time, General Harry Haystead looked directly at Jasmine Jones. The Chinese girl hadn't moved from her post at the office door, and all that could be heard for a moment was the sibilant hissing of an air-conditioning system operating somewhere. Durell wondered if everything that had been said was recorded on tape and film. He had the feeling, bred into him by so many similar circumstances, of being watched and studied by unseen eyes. Something flickered across Haystead's flat boyish face as he studied the tall girl.

"You," he said to her. "You work for McFee, is that right?"

"Yes, sir."

"I must tell you I didn't want you in on this at all. But we all have to compromise, unfortunately. That's the trouble with this sort of thing. That's how people get killed." He paused. "Your orders are with Durell's. He'll brief you. I think your presence is unnecessary. But it can't be helped. All right, then. I guess that's all."

Durell did not move. Haystead lifted hard brows at him. "Is something the matter? I said you could go."

"Everything is the matter. I want to know who and what I'm really working for. You've talked a lot of garbage about treason in high places, General Haystead, all tied in with this Nationalist, Chien Y-Wu, now in Peking. I don't think I have enough to do this job."

"You have all I can give you," Haystead said decisively. He smiled suddenly, and again the fanatic light of discipline became a boyish grin in his pale eyes. "You're not going to back out on me, are you?"

Every instinct in Durell told him that he should, right now. But his instinct also told him that he would be a dead man, one way or the other, if he gave Haystead the wrong answer. He felt suddenly like an innocent target caught in a field of cross fire. Or a tool, a cat's-paw, for people and purposes he could only dimly perceive. It was too late, definitely, to back out now.

Haystead offered him a quick, politician's hand. "Good luck, Durell. Be careful. And I will see you here in three weeks. With Chien, or with proof of his death. We can't give you any more time than that."

He looked at Jasmine with hostility. "And you, Miss Jones, may tell McFee what you like."

Six

JASMINE WENT DIRECTLY TO THE BEDROOM OF THE small suite reserved for Durell at the Sea Goddess Hotel and left the door only slightly ajar. The night was warm. Durell lit one of his rare cigarettes, drew the draperies across the sliding glass balcony doors, shutting off the sight of the pool and the main lobby. Music came dimly from the cocktail terrace down there. He heard the sounds of the Chinese girl moving about in the next room, but he did not go in to see her; they had spoken very little to each other on the drive back from General Haystead's office.

Durell took the thin file of briefing notes and put them flat on the coffee table, switched on a modern bull's-eye reading lamp, and started going through the sheets of thin, finely typed papers in the folder. They had been classified 4-AX—to be read and destroyed.

The first sheet dealt with his projected flight to mainland China with Colonel Chu. Haystead, he admitted reluctantly, was as efficient as the top-secret computers and code breakers in the lower basements of the National Security Agency's headquarters outside of Washington.

Every possible contingency seemed to be provided for, although Durell was skeptical of such carefully calculated plans. Men did not act like machines or according to the rules of higher mathematics. The details of such a project as this rarely worked out as proposed. Disaster could arise from a slip on the smallest detail—and no one could foresee what such a detail might be.

It could turn upon a suspicious traffic cop or shop-keeper, a drunk reeling down a street, a delay in a railway schedule, illness, the weather, a thousand and one trivialities to delay or upset such a tightly worked schedule.

Nevertheless, Durell studied and memorized the names of all contacts he might need en route, contingency hide-outs, alternate passages, a highly detailed map of Peking, a description of the house in which the Nationalist general Chien Y-Wu, was being held. He had been trained for this sort of mental discipline, and after scanning the page twice he had the capacity of visual recall to read off, as if the instructions were before his eyes, every word he had just read.

He lit a match and burned this first sheet with care in a large stone ashtray, crushed the ashes into black powder, and then turned to the dossiers and attached photographs.

```
ZA55/Proj.7b.2/CLASSIFIED 4/ANALYST 5B
WARNING: READ AND DESTROY.
    CHIEN, Y-Wu, Brig. General, Nationalist Chinese
Army, KMT, Commander Lotus Dept. E. Branch.
    Age: 44
    Phys. Descrip: Hgt: 5'8" Wgt: 220. Dist.
Mks: Wears steel-rimmed reading glasses constantly.
No other identities except bayonet scar left side
chin.
    Marital Status: Two wives, Taipei; 7 children.
    Comments: General Chien a close intimate at
one time of the Generalissimo and ruling hierarchy
Kuomintang.  In the years immediately preceding the
defeat by Mao Tse-tung's Red Army forces and sub-
sequent flight of the Nationalist Army to Formosa,
was close to ruling circles.  For a time, out of favor
afterward in Taipei as result of slack discipline
```

and defeat of commanded division. Tried and judged
for loose morale in troops leading to defection and
surrender of approx. 6,000 men before the retreat to
Formosa. Acquitted 1948, demoted to lt. colonel,
given duty U.S.A. at Cipher Dept. V, 1949-1953.
Engaged by Dept. V for info source, received training under Brig. Gen. H. H. Haystead in electronic
data-collection, code analysis, and since has been
receiving personal emoluments which have been de-
posited his name Suisse Banque Nationale, Geneva.
Total amount to July 1968: $107,505.   Fund 22.

   Critical Data: Although some areas doubt exist
in re subject's opportunism, he has performed ex-
cellently in guiding and gathering mainland China's
economic and industrial military establishment
under Zebra flight program. His vanishment 17 June
with no further direct word from subject is a matter
of critical and urgent policy decision. His information on U.S. electronic capacity and Zebra program
could if divulged to Peking's L-5, create enormous
tensions for the KMT government on Taiwan, with
hostilities a 98% developed conclusion.

   URGENT: It must be learned immediately whether
Chien Y-Wu was captured against his wish or if he
voluntarily defected. No trace of Zebra aircraft
57.Z can be located. Info received indicates subject
presently quartered in Black House at Peking, living
with a woman, presently unidentified. His family
relations in Taipei indicate no marital or domestic
difficulties.

   Chien must be rescued or eliminated.

   See attached Photo 72752 and accompanying data.

   Durell turned to the next dossier and read about the
man he was to impersonate.

   ZA55/Proj.7b.3/CLASSIFIED 4/ANALYST 65/File
L-5-1212:

   SHAN, Tze Peng, Major, People's Army of the
Chinese Republic, assigned L-5 Black House 1962 to
present date.

   General Data: Born 1924, joined Long March as a
boy, a devoted Marxist and Communist ideologist,
educated U. of Peking, electronics engineering, Wu-

han KPI Industrial Communal Factory 4. Transferred
to Manchuria, 1964, married, wife died 1967, assigned to Taipei and entered island via Hong Kong
with cover as transistor manufacturer. Identified
as Black House agent on 21 June 1968, by General
Chien, reported to Zebra and Lotus Groups. Kept
under surveillance two months to learn contacts.
Results negative and ordered eliminated by Colonel
Chu of Lotus Group 2. Reports continue to be sent
in Shan's name to L-5 Peking to date.

Critical Data: It was recently learned by Lotus
via Zebra that Shan Tze Peng is being ordered back
to Peking for report and indoctrination to and in
Six Sentinel Group. No data on meaning of Six
Sentinels; no data on such program. No data on
Shan's superiors in Black House. Agents Ling and
Barkovsky killed in Peking. No data returned.

URGENT: Code 7/BZ5--The replacement of Shan
considered highly speculative and unpromising project. Analysis indicates 87.6% failure projection.

Durell considered the last sentence for a long moment,
his face without expression, and then he burned the on-
ionskin, crushed the ashes, and took up the last two
items.

Precis, Henry Talbot-Smythe, liaison officer
Sigma, K Section, State Department, Division of
Analysis and Projection:

Information in regard to K Section's recent
activities in the Far East indicates several dangerous and provocative moves against the militant
Peking Army groups, unfavorably regarded by Con-
gressional Committee (Harrison), Defense Department, Division of Chinese Affairs, and Joint Chiefs.
Chief instigator of these moves is believed to be
General Dickinson McFee, of the autonomous K Section
of the Central Intelligence Agency.

Reports from our Oriental experts express alarm
at these provocative acts that may precipitate armed
hostilities against the Taiwan regime.

It is recommended that General McFee be removed
from command of K Section and that this unit be dis-

banded and its personnel debriefed and assigned to
NSA wherever favorably indicated.

Confidential Memo 27/0
From: White Guard
To: Dragon
Subject: D.McF., K Sec.
      Who and what are the Six Sentinels? It has come
to the attention of the President and he requests
immediate and definitive data. There is no compre-
hensive file on Zebra Program, Lotus Group 2, or the
subject commanding K Section. It is noted that
White House directives and public statements of
policy have often been directly contravened by both
overt and sub rosa activities. Preliminary inves-
tigation indicates the source of these provocations
can be and must be a result of subject's independent
activities.
      This can be a threat to the safety and defense of
the nation.
      In the critical case of General Chien, subject's
field agent has been transferred to the direct command of Zebra.
      It is believed that the Six Sentinels represent
a highly secret military and political group seeking international provocations in order to achieve
a domestic coup d'etat in Washington and establishment of a junta. Identities must be discovered at
all costs, the soonest.

      Durell burned the last of the papers, then added the
thin folder to the heap of black, crushed ashes. He picked
up the heavy stone ashtray, took it into the elaborately
tiled bath, flushed the ashes down the toilet, cleaned the
tray, and returned it to the living room. There was a faint
scent of spicy feminine perfume in the air, an essence of
femininity that made him look toward the bedroom door.
A dim light glowed there. But no sound came from the
bedroom.
      He walked to the door and pushed it all the way open
with his fingertips. Jasmine lay in the king-size bed, with
only a sheet over her naked body. She had loosened her
long black hair, and it lay shimmering about her head on

the white pillow. Her eyes were closed, but her face reflected tension, even fear. There was a rigidity to her body and her long, exposed legs that also told him much about her state of mind, and he made his voice gentle when he spoke.

"It's all right, Jasmine."

She spoke without opening her eyes. "No, it is not all right."

"What's wrong, then?"

"Your voice is Sam Durell's, but when I look at you——"

He smiled. "Did Ike Greentree make me so ugly?"

"No."

"Is it because I now look Chinese?"

"Yes."

"But you're Chinese."

"Yes. And I'm all mixed up about it."

He took off his clothes and turned out the light and sat on the edge of the bed beside her. "It's dark now. You can't see my face. Is that better?"

A thin breath escaped her parted lips. He kissed her. She did not respond at all and he said, "What is it? Tell me, Jasmine. We can't have any secrets between us."

"I know what you're thinking, Sam dear."

"And what is that?"

"You think that McFee insisted and managed to get agreement that I go with you so he could be informed about you. It must be plain to you that General Haystead has accepted me on this assignment very reluctantly."

"Yes, that's true," Durell said.

"So you know that I'm a defense mechanism put into the works by General McFee."

"He doesn't need any defense from me," Durell said.

"But he said you might be influenced otherwise. So in a sense, he insisted that I go along to spy on you."

"Yes, I understand that. Surveillance is a fact of life in this business."

"Are you not angry with me?"

"No. We all have our jobs to do. What else do you know about the situation?"

"Nothing," Jasmine said, in a way that told him she knew more.

"Do you think that matters may develop in such a way that I may have to decide to kill McFee?"

"Perhaps," she said. "No one knows much about him, I think. Or the whole thing may be a trap, Sam dear. I think you have been selected as some kind of sacrificial lamb to appease some hidden power somewhere." Her voice changed a little. "But you are not a paper tiger, Sam. I know the terrible things you can and have done."

"Do you trust Colonel Chu?" he asked suddenly.

Her answer was prompt. "No. Not at all."

"Good girl. Be suspicious. It's the only way to survive in this business."

"Do you trust me?" she asked.

"No. Not a bit."

He slid into bed with her, drew aside the sheet over her waist, and held her long, firm body close to him. She kept her limbs rigid for a moment, and then with a gasp she tangled her long legs with his and turned to him and made herself utterly fluid against him. He felt the cool slide of sudden tears on her cheeks.

"You are not in love with me," she whispered. "You love Deirdre Padgett."

He made no answer. Her hands slid over his chest and downward, and he felt a quick stir of response in him. It had been a long time, from Singapore to Taipei, since he had been with a girl like this.

He accepted her then as she accepted him, lovers for the moment, but with a dark area of reserve, danger, and suspicion between them.

Seven

IT WAS THREE HOURS BEFORE DAWN. THERE WAS A cool dampness in the air, as if it were going to rain soon. The military airfield was shrouded in darkness except for the winking green and red and amber lights and the fluorescent lighting from the glass-enclosed control tower. The shadows of coveralled men moved silently around the needle-nosed jets on the strips, and the planes looked like giant, vicious insects with their dark, eager shapes poised against the black night.

Colonel Chu had picked up Durell and Jasmine in a closed, air-conditioned limousine. The KMT flyer had little to say this morning. His manner had changed and he was engrossed in his own thoughts and plans and the dangerous problem of the flight over the mainland. He was crisp and efficient in checking out the light D-5 Zebra jet, a new type for high-altitude flights, with enormously long wings and a fragile, narrow fuselage. It was an unfamiliar plane to Durell, without markings of any kind, and it was equipped with long, whiplike antennae and a radar dome with its detection and listening equipment.

"Can we get to Peking before dawn in this?" Durell asked.

"There will be no problem about that, Major Shan."

"That's what you hope."

"Yes, there must always be hope, and a little luck, in anything like this."

They were given parachute equipment by the Chinese airmen and oxygen masks for their high-altitude drop. In a small room in the hangar, Durell and Jasmine were made to change their clothing: he into a mainland Chinese suit, and she into a dress manufactured in Peking. They were given identity papers, railroad passes, and enough currency and change to amply take care of them. Durell didn't know if the money was forged or not. Chu came in while Durell was knotting his wide necktie and gave him a small Chinese revolver that slid smoothly into a small pocket inside the coarse jacket he wore.

"I don't think I should be armed," Durell said.

"Major Shan always carried this. It was his. And the clothing you are putting on was his, too. Even to the shoes."

"Yes, they're tight. A dead man's shoes."

Chu smiled thinly. "You are not superstitious, Shan?

We Chinese think of ourselves as having a monopoly on that." He looked at the plane, adjusted his complicated and burdensome flying gear, and added, "Well, I suppose we are ready. Climb aboard."

There was nothing to see, nothing to hear but the whine of the jet engines. Now and then the plane bumped and shivered, and the long wings lifted and fell in a birdlike flapping motion. Jasmine was silent and self-contained in her bucket seat. Durell occupied a monitor's chair in the cockpit beside Chu, who flew the plane with an easy and effortless appearance of efficiency. Only a small dim navigating light shone over the instruments and the knee-type calculator strapped to the colonel's leg. Now and then Chu yawned. Durell wondered if the occasional buffeting of the plane was getting on the man's nerves.

There was no sign of interception or detection of their flight. No missiles streaked up to greet them from the continental land mass shrouded under the cloud cover beneath the jet. Then the plane lurched again and Jasmine made a little sound. Durell looked at her. Her black almond eyes were wide and questioning.

A clicking noise came from the mass of detection gear in the narrow fuselage aft. Chu turned his head sharply.

"We are being monitored. They have caught us."

"Can we evade?"

"I shall try."

"How near are we to Peking?" Durell asked.

"We are only above Wuhan. On the Yangstze River."

"That's impossible. That puts us far east of Nanking, off course hundreds of miles inland." Durell was suddenly angry. "I thought we'd be cutting across the East China Sea."

"I only follow orders. Zebra flights are commanded by Lotus Group 2." Chu sounded irritable. "We must obey orders, eh? Even when they seem senseless."

The clicking came faster, with an ominous note in the mechanical sound. Chu put the plane into a sharp port bank and dived. The wings shuddered. There was a faint light in the sky now, although they had been racing away from the dawn over Taiwan. There were more bumps, and a flare of light burst with yellow and red in the cloud layer down below. Chu's mouth tightened. There was a desperate look in his eyes.

"Is it bad?" Durell asked quietly.

"This was not supposed to happen," Chu complained.

"Nothing ever goes according to plan."

"But it was arranged—it was not to happen!"

Durell's voice was dry. "Do you mean we've been betrayed—already?"

"Perhaps. I do not know. Be prepared to jump soon. You will need your oxygen."

"We're still a long way from Peking."

Chu snapped, "Well, you will just have to make the best of it."

Durell reached back to help Jasmine arrange her breathing gear. She had a strange little smile on her moist lips. Something flashed past the cockpit window and the plane lurched, tipped, and spun down. Suddenly the world was blotted out by clouds; but they would be of no protection against the tracking gear that had caught them. Jasmine lowered her eyes when he stared at her, wondering about her inward smile. Then she looked up as if she were about to tell him something, and then nodded toward Chu. Durell shook his head and helped her from the bucket seat.

Chu rasped out their instructions for the jump. There was another burst of light off the port wing. The plane was lower now. They had to wait an interminable minute, then another. Jasmine was to jump first. The small door in the rear, just forward of the bulging radar dome, was ready for them as they made their way aft in the plane.

"Good luck!" Chu called. "Count five!"

Durell did not reply. A light went on and a door slid shut between them and the pilot's compartment, to prevent decompression up forward. Then the door popped open. Jasmine braced herself with both hands, but couldn't bring herself to jump into the roaring maelstrom of air. Durell abruptly shoved her out, saw her body tumble into gray, cloudy space, and stepped out himself.

For long minutes he let himself go in free fall. He could see nothing but the dim clouds. He was aware of intense cold, even through the insulated suit he wore— and which he would have to destroy, or use another cover story if he were spotted in it. After the proper count, he pulled the chute ring. He had lost sight of Jasmine. There was a jolt, and his fall was checked. He looked up and saw a violent burst and explosion in the sky above and wondered if Chu and the plane had been hit. Then he concentrated on his own safe landing.

For a long minute or two, he could see only the grayish mist of clouds, a slowly turning sky that grew pearly with the dawn light. It seemed to him that Chu would have been late for a drop in the Peking vicinity anyway, and perhaps this had all been arranged—but by whom, or for what reason, he couldn't guess.

Suddenly the mass of the earth loomed below, dark and shrouded with night mists, with a gleam of faint lights here and there that did not form a definite pattern. They were not city lights, so he wasn't over Wuhan, he thought gratefully. It also occurred to him that he had only Colonel Chu's word for their position anyway.

He saw a low range of bare hills, indefinite and misty, a flat pattern of fields, a strip of road, a gleam of water, the dark density of woods off to the right. He manipulated the chute toward the wooded area and tried to turn in all directions to see if he could spot Jasmine. She was not in sight, and he felt a deep clutch of anxiety about her. Then the fields and woods came up with an accelerating rush that, despite previous jumps, he had never been able to adjust to.

He hit hard, felt a jolt in his left leg, rolled over several times; unidentified objects battered at his body. Almost at once, however, he was up and gathering in the bright shrouds of lines to the nylon chute. The mass of the woods was only a hundred yards away. He had landed in one of the fields and fallen once over a rickety wooden fence. He could see no houses nearby, for which he was grateful.

Pausing, he stood very still and listened, but there was

no sound through the drifting mist of dawn. So his landing had not yet attracted any alarm. No one was in sight. Nothing moved anywhere. The rich, pungent smell of turned earth stung his nostrils as he stripped off the oxygen gear and the jump suit, gathered in the suit with swift, strong tugs on the cords, and then made his way toward the shelter of the nearby trees.

All the equipment that might have identified him was especially made for easy destruction. He walked far enough into the forest to be sure nothing could be detected from the fields, and struck a wooden match to light the material. The chute, cords, and jump suit vanished in a quick hiss of flameless chemical destruction. The metal parts of his equipment he had to bury, and this took some moments of groping in the dark gloom between the trees. The air was cool and damp, but he sweated as he worked to dispose of all traces of his origin.

Ten minutes later there was nothing left to identify him as anyone but Major Shan Tze Peng. He tried to make himself think now in Chinese, in the language he would have to use. He drew a deep breath and walked out of the woods to look across the gray horizon of flat fields.

"Jasmine?" he called softly.

There was no answer.

He called louder, "Jasmine!"

There was no sign of her. Not a trace. He had not seen her chute open. He hadn't seen her land. He didn't know if she was alive or dead, or where she might be.

For that matter, Durell thought grimly, he didn't know where he was, either. And if he made one slip from this moment on, there would be no question about his future.

He would be a dead man.

Eight

HE SPENT AN HOUR HUNTING FOR JASMINE, BUT there was no sign of her. She could have come down

miles away, of course. And she knew their contact in
Wuhan. By the time he gave up the search, it was broad
daylight. A mist lay in the hollows of the fields, but the
sun rapidly burned away these patches of fog. Here and
there a pond shimmered in the morning light, and he
heard the distant cackling of geese. He had checked the
edges of the wood, coursing and traversing the area for
half a mile in each direction. Jasmine had disappeared.
True, she had been trained for this drop, and she knew
how to make herself invisible in the countryside, and
since there was no sign that her drop had been unsuccess-
ful, he had to assume she was still alive. But she had not
taken the planned measures for meeting, which meant,
perhaps, that she had wanted to vanish.

Far off to the west, perhaps two miles away, he saw a
smudge of chimney smoke. It could be charcoal burners,
he thought, and he began to walk that way across the
plowed fields, crossing fences here and there. He limped a
little, and his leg ached where he had bruised it when he
landed. Walking soon eased the soreness out of it, however. The sun grew hotter, and the fields steamed and
smelled with the rank smell of an alien culture.

In less than a mile he came to a dirt road, and he followed this toward the thin finger of smoke that stained
the pale sky. So far he hadn't seen a human being, which
didn't make him feel easier. So much, he thought, for
China's overcrowded population. A brooding silence filled
the world, as if he had landed in a place from which all
the inhabitants had recently fled. It could be possible, he
thought, and took off his stiff Peking jacket and slung it
over his arm. In his hand under the coat he kept his gun
ready.

If Colonel Chu had been shot down in his pterodactyl
plane, there was no more sign of him than there was of
Jasmine.

After another half hour he heard a train whistle from
somewhere ahead. He quickened his step, topped a rise,
and saw his first house. It was a peasant's farm compound, and he heard pigs grunting and the clucking of
chickens. The farm animals were running loose. The

house was built in the old style, with a walled court, thatched roofs, tiled walks. He moved more carefully. The smoke came from here, but it was neither a chimney fire nor charcoal burners. Half the house had been burned down, and the rest was smoldering and gutted.

He paused, swearing softly, and checked himself to think in Mandarin before he called, "Good morning!"

Something made a scrabbling sound inside the recent ruin, but he didn't think it was an animal. As he stepped up to the door, a low moan of terror greeted him.

"Hello, mother," he said gently. "I will not hurt you. Do not be afraid."

She was very old and wrinkled, which was why the marauders had left her alone. He felt a brief pang of fear for Jasmine, and dismissed it. The old woman wore a blue smock, and had her gray hair pulled back in a tight, skinned knot. There was a dribble of blood on her lips and chin.

"Mother, tell me what happened here."

"Who—who are you?" Her Mandarin, surprisingly, was tolerable.

"I am Major Shan Tze Peng. I'm looking for the railroad.

"Shan?"

"That is my name."

Her black eyes rounded with fear. "They came looking for you."

"For me?"

"Truly. They asked if we had seen you. They took my man, my son, my two daughters—"

"Who were they?" he asked quietly.

"Soldiers!" she spat. There was a depth of contempt and loathing in her wise eyes that reflected a lifetime of terror.

He moved into the doorway, wondering if he were being watched; the old woman wiped the blood from her chin and walked to a kerosene stove. An iron pot of rice was still hot there. She said, "It is not as if we are disloyal to the government. We live better now than in the old days. But my husband happens to be old-fashioned, sir. We live by the old rules. Still, our children are gone. They march and wander over the countryside, and this old woman's heart is broken. Now they have taken my last son."

"When did the soldiers come?" he asked.

"At sunrise."

"And you are sure they asked for me, for Shan?"

She nodded, suspicious of him. "Are you a criminal? Have you said or done anything to displease the State?"

"No, mother. May I have some of that rice?"

"You are welcome."

He ate quietly and quickly. The pigs and chickens settled down outside. The old Chinese woman watched him. When he was finished he thanked her and said, "Was there a young woman with the soldiers, mother?"

"Several," she said contemptuously.

"A tall girl, beautiful——"

"I had no time to see beauty when my home was burning," she said.

"Of course. I'm sorry. I will leave you now."

There was a village a short distance down the road. People were still there, working at a fish pond. He saw no soldiers, but decided to give the commune a wide berth and moved off through a small, carefully gleaned wood. After another hour, he came to the outskirts of a larger town. The day was very hot now, with a breathless quality in the still air. He followed a telephone line back to the main road and soon came to more houses and decided there was no help for it, he had to appear in public. He quickened his pace, walking briskly as if he had an official errand to perform.

The people on the streets paid no attention to him. He wished he knew the name of the town, but he didn't ask, and suddenly he saw the gleam of railroad tracks and followed them until he came to the station on the south side of the settlement. He was sweating, but it was not from the heat of the day. He knew his city clothes must stand out among these country folk, and he knew his presence had been noted a score of times. No help for that, he thought. The whole assignment had the aura of disaster and certainly of treachery.

He had the proper papers, a railway pass with his photo on it, a priority card for passage to Peking, and enough money to ease his way. No one seemed to be interested in him, however. The railroad station consisted of a long wooden platform and a modern cinder-block ticket office and waiting rooms with upturned red roof tiles. It was crowded with round-faced, blank-eyed peasants, both men and women and children, all cleanly dressed in the countryside's uniform outfit of a blue half-coat and pants and sneakers. There were only two men in railroad uniforms, and a few bespectacled officials in Western-type clothing like his own.

The station sign indicating the name of the town meant nothing to him, but another sign showing that the big industrial center of Wuhan was only one hundred miles away turned out to be comforting.

He drew a deep breath then and walked boldly into the press of waiting peasants and crossed the platform to the ticket office. Round black eyes followed him curiously. A cluster of loudspeakers began to blare out martial music, loud enough to numb the mind. A hawker selling a poisonous-looking orange drink barred his way for a moment, then shrugged and turned aside.

The ticket collector was a sharp-faced woman from Manchuria. She scarcely glanced at his credentials.

"You have priority, of course, Comrade Shan, but the train to Wuhan has been delayed. There has been some —difficulty."

"I understand. When will the train arrive now?"

"In an hour, Comrade Shan." She looked up at him. It was hard to read what moved behind her eyes; but something was there. Over the blaring speakers, which now gave out with an impassioned anti-American, anti-imperialist, anti-capitalist warmonger speech, the female stationmaster tried to smile. Durell had seen better grimaces on the faces of the dead. "Comrade, you are too important to be kept waiting among these people. We have orders to make you comfortable. Please come this way."

"I am gratified," he said courteously, "but I am also curious. Was I expected?"

The woman blinked. "Of course, Comrade Shan."

He saw out of the corner of his eye several uniformed People's Police moving toward him, automatic weapons slung on their shoulders. He decided to accept the stationmaster's invitation and murmured, "You are most kind. It is most correct behavior for a member of our glorious People's Republic."

"Use the door to the left," she said sharply.

There was a long corridor that bisected the station building. Who expected him? And why? he wondered. But so much for top-secret assignments. The uniformed woman appeared behind him and led him unsmilingly down the bleak, white station hall. Telegraph keys chattered from behind one of the doors. The blaring propaganda speech was repeated from the loudspeakers in the ceiling, but no one seemed to be listening to it.

"In here, Comrade."

She opened the door and stepped back a little too quickly. The room beyond looked shadowed, with blinds drawn down over the utilitarian windows. Durell had no choice but to go in. The shadow of a man loomed to his right. He stepped sidewise, used his elbow, chopped at the wrist of the hand that held the glint of a gun, stabbed at the man's side with stiff fingers, and dropped to his knees, all in one swift, blindingly fluid movement. The man gave a stifled scream and staggered into a steel desk, folded over it, and began vomiting. Then something whipped over Durell's head as he ducked, came up, and kicked backward at a second soldier's kneecap. There was a crack of bone and cartilage, very satisfying. Then he saw the first man lift himself up, round face spasmed with pain, and level a revolver at him.

The picture changed abruptly. They were not out to capture him alive. They meant to kill him. Death lurked in a dark pool behind the man's eyes.

Durell's gun was in his hand like swift magic. In the same instant, he knew he couldn't fire. The sound would turn the whole station into an uproar. But the soldier didn't think of this; he froze and swallowed loudly.

"Exactly," Durell said softly. "Or you are a dead man."

"And who shall speak for you, Comrade Shan, from the grave?" came another voice.

Durell backed up slowly until his shoulders were against the wall. He kicked the first soldier's weapon across the room. The second soldier had fainted from the pain of his broken knee. Then he looked for the third man.

In today's Chinese People's Republic, there were not many fat men. And this one was not merely fat. He was enormous in all dimensions, crowding a side door that opened into an adjacent station office. He wore a Russian-style double-breasted serge suit that bulged and stretched and strained about his massive shoulders and enormous arms and belly. His necktie was wide and florid.

The Chinese spoke in soft, impeccable Mandarin. "Welcome back to the homeland, Major Shan."

Durell wondered if he was supposed to recognize this monster of a man. He kept his voice impersonal.

"The welcome is not what I expected, after so many long years of faithful duty abroad," he said. "You seem to have been expecting me."

"Of course."

"I was not aware of another apparatus in Taipei."

"Naturally. We have none." The man may have smiled, but it was difficult to tell. His big face folded and creased; his naked, bald scalp wrinkled; but nothing changed in his black, slitted eyes. "I am here only to hasten your return to the Black House, where we look forward to your report on the American imperialist warmongering organization known as the Six Sentinels."

There was no Oriental lack of directness here, Durell thought grimly. He decided he had to take a chance and said, "Comrade, we have never met before."

"A thousand apologies. My name is Tai Ma Cho."

The big Chinese face was direct, bleak, inquisitive. The

two injured soldiers were quiet, except for an occasional groan. Tai Ma Cho did not even seem to know they existed.

"You are fortunate," he said, "that we found you first, Shan. We have many enemies, and not all of them are abroad, as you must know. The others look for you and will not let you live. But you are safe now. The train will be here in fifteen minutes, and in the meantime we shall drink tea together."

"Both in the motherland and among our foreign enemies," Durell said quietly, "there are two parallel lines. One is sane. The other is headed by madmen. And each line connects on the sublime horizon of Pe._.g." He smiled to remove any sting from his archaic expression.

Tai Ma Cho nodded seriously. "Proletarian truths are self-evident. And which of those who smile among us are our enemies is a question we shall answer soon, with your help. Please, come this way."

The huge man gestured Durell through the doorway. There wasn't much room to squeeze past his bulk, and this did not give Durell much leverage when, in squeezing by, he slammed his left fist into the big, hard belly, kicked with his right heel at the fat man's ankle, and then dived forward into the other room. Tai Ma grunted and lifted an arm that came down on the back of Durell's neck like a poleax. Durell fell on his knees, rolled around a steel desk, came up and started for the window. Tai Ma was shouting in a thin, furious voice. A shot crashed, and the bullet screamed off the steel desk top. He glimpsed the other's face and had no doubt now that the whole setup was designed to execute him quietly and without fuss. The desperate shot ended that part of the plan. There were shouts from outside the station house, and the blaring loudspeaker went up a number of decibels as someone had the initiative to try to drown out the sounds of murder.

Durell risked a glimpse above the desk that sheltered him. There was a window across the room and a brick wall opposite, indicating an alley about five feet wide. There was a hissing, clacking conversation from the doorway. The man from the Black House had retreated to the safety of the outer room.

"Major Shan!"

Durell kept silent. It was always best to let the opposition guess and wonder. He weighed his chances of reaching the window safely. They were just about nil. And yet there was no other way out. Every second was important; he could hear Tai Ma Cho calling urgently for more men. The window would be covered soon and then his back would be exposed, too, with the desk made useless to him. A light, cold sweat made his shirt cling to his back.

There was a stone paperweight on the desktop. He reached up with one hand, caught it, and threw it toward the doorway. A rapid series of muffled, silenced shots made the stone bounce, chip, and split apart. So much for that, he thought bitterly.

He had been betrayed from just about every direction. The dark strands of the conspiracy stretched all the way back to Taipei and beyond, all the way to Washington and a number of faceless figures there. He did not know how or why he had been chosen as a scapegoat, or just what he was supposed or not supposed to accomplish for either side in this formless and as yet inchoate web of intrigue. His anger flared against McFee—one of the betrayers?—for not filling him in more accurately or honestly. But this line of thought was no help just now, he decided. The seconds were flying by too fast.

Footsteps clattered in the outer room. There was a hurried conversation in Mandarin, pitched low and not clear enough to understand. Again Durell estimated the distance to the window. And when he looked at it, he saw Jasmine Jones' face there.

It was only a fleeting glimpse. She wore a peasant's wide, conical straw hat and what seemed like the usual blue coolie jacket. He saw an arm come up, something flew into the room where he was trapped, and there followed a shattering blast of smoke and glass and acrid fumes.

"Shan!"

Her voice was high, shrill, imperative. Smoke rolled

from the shattered doorway. He did not know if the fat Chinese was alive or dead—and did not care. He lifted to one knee, spun on his heel, and dived through the window, shattering the remaining glass. He fell a bit farther than expected, landed on outstretched hands, rolled over once, came up against a wall with a thump, and was instantly on his feet, crouching.

"This way, Shan!"

He followed Jasmine's voice. Flames shot through the window, and there were distant shouts and whistles. To his right, the alley followed the station building, under tiled eaves, to the glinting railroad tracks. He thought he heard a locomotive whistle in the distance, but he could not be sure, with all the noises of alarm around him. In the other direction, the alley opened on the street. He did not see Jasmine, but he turned that way, and in half a dozen steps Jasmine came from a niche in the wall and fell in stride with him. She pulled at his arm.

"The other way—the train to Wuhan——"

"No."

"But we must get to Wuhan!"

"Shut up," he said.

He looked back. Two soldiers tumbled through the shattered stationhouse window. They blocked the way to the tracks, and the decision was made for them. Jasmine ran with him into the street. Other people were running, too, in all directions. That made it easier. Jasmine had done well for herself, he noted, one part of his mind curiously alert to her. She had found a People's Guard uniform and now wore it easily, the baggy shirt and trousers not concealing her lithe form; her black hair was tucked up under the curious little militia cap. She also carried a heavy revolver in a holster, which was banging at her hip.

"That way." She pointed toward a street of shops.

"You know your way around," he said dryly.

"I had some time, waiting for you to show up."

"You had no trouble with the landing?"

"No."

"I couldn't find you, Jasmine."

She was silent. Her manner was tight. They passed a

soup stall, and the cooking odors and charcoal smoke made him suddenly aware of his hunger. He looked back over his shoulder; there was no apparent pursuit. Jasmine deftly threaded her way through the chattering people, holding his hand, occasionally tugging him this way or that.

"The train usually stops a few hundred yards out of the station to debark Red Guard platoons and others," she said. "We have our tickets, anyway. They won't expect us to be on the train *already*."

She was clever enough. And it worked out exactly as she suggested. Within two minutes, they saw the locomotive, chuffing at a siding. Young boys and girls were tumbling off. Some were armed, some wore school uniforms, others were in nondescript dungarees and sneakers. All had a fanatical but disciplined bearing as they responded to their flag-waving leaders. No others were at the siding. Jasmine and Durell walked casually to the second coach from the locomotive and swung aboard, pushing against the tide of young people coming off. None glanced at them. After all, Durell thought wryly, he looked as Chinese as any of them.

But as he swung aboard he felt something hard in his back, and he did not need to turn to know it was a gun. And Jasmine held it on him.

He paused in the empty vestibule, and saw her as if she were a stranger, her face hard and bleak and alien.

"You, too, Jasmine?"

"I'm sorry, Sam."

"I've been betrayed all around, is that it?"

"You know it," she said quietly. "From here on, you do exactly as I say. I don't know where you've been or what you've been up to since we jumped from Chu's plane —and you know what my job really is."

"So much for loving me."

"I have a job to do."

"So do I," he said. "Would you kill me, if you had to?"

"Don't," she said bitterly, "make me decide about that."

Nine

DURELL WATCHED A YOUNG WOMAN DUST AND polish the floors and windows of the coach while the train jolted toward Wuhan. The public-address system crackled endlessly with exhortations to keep the train clean and work for socialism; occasionally, scheduled stops were announced, along with food facilities at the various stations. There were folk songs, an occasional military chorus, frequent diatribes against Western imperialists. Once, for fifteen minutes, there was a screeching Chinese opera solo, and Jasmine reached under the window and turned a knob to cut off the sound.

"We may be suspect for not listening to patriotic songs," she said, "but I can't stand my own country's music."

He stared at her. "Is this your true country, Jasmine?"

"You know I'm San Francisco-born. But I'm still one of these people."

"Put away your gun," he said. "It makes me nervous. Take your hand out of your pocket."

She smiled. "Are you angry?"

"Let me see both hands or I'll kill you," he said.

"How can we work together, if you——"

They were interrupted by a girl attendant in blue cotton, with a duster cloth over her black hair. She smiled, showing strong white teeth, and wiped soot from the window ledge, then took two mugs and small packets of green tea and poured hot water for them. The tea was weak and tasteless. It was hot in the train, and the sun glared off lush paddy fields and distant hills. The passengers chattered loudly in the overcrowded compartments, and their talk was not overheard.

"We were lucky," she said. "Can't you see that? I'm sorry if you don't trust me, but I couldn't take a chance.

McFee ordered me to make sure you—to see that you—
—" She shook her head. "I can't tell you more. I'm just
supposed to watch you, that's all, and make sure you
don't—meet the wrong people."

He tried to read her eyes, but her thick lashes came
down as she drank her tea, and he sighed and stared
through the window. The assignment, he thought, had
been betrayed from the start. He could trust no one—not
Haystead, who gave the orders, nor McFee. But he had
to go on. It was a lonely feeling.

Twenty minutes later, the train halted at a shabby village, and platoons of regular soldiers came aboard. The
officer swaggered through the coach, glaring at everyone.
Durell yawned and settled lower on his spine. Jasmine
drank her tea. Outside, there were fields with green crops,
small clumps of newly planted trees. The people who
came and went during the brief halt wore simple blue cotton suits; a few women had on cheap floral dresses. The
loudspeaker blared interminably, and when the officer
stared at them, Jasmine turned up the volume control
under their window. The soldier nodded, smiled, and
walked on.

"Was he looking for us?" Jasmine whispered.

"I doubt it. They don't believe we got on the train."

"Sooner or later, they'll know it and telegraph ahead."

"We'll be in Wuhan in another hour."

He felt trapped as the train rocked and chuffed across
the countryside. The ancient way of life in the fields still
persisted. He saw peasant women with lampshade hats,
fringed with black cotton against the harsh sun; boys rode
water buffalo and splashed in the irrigation canals; carts
with rubber tires were pushed laboriously along dusty
lanes; and each village platform was mobbed with crowds
jostling around the food carts.

"Sam?"

"Keep your hands in sight."

"Please, Sam. I had to do it. Don't be angry with me."
She paused. "Please trust me."

"I don't. Not until you level with me."

Her black, slanted eyes glistened. He did not believe

anything she might say. Someone had sold the project down the river from the start; the enemy had been waiting for him. He did not know who to trust or turn to, but again, he saw no choice except to go on.

Wuhan was a sprawling industrial complex, including the cities of Hankow, Hanyang, and Wuchang, hundreds of miles inland from the mouth of the vast Yangtze River. There was smog over it from the ship-building, chemical, and textile factories, as well as the new huge steel bridge that spanned the river. There were western-style hotels, like the Victory, and the new, enormous Yang Cheng. The train slowed though newly built workers' housing, like barracks, low factories, and some of the old slums left by German and Japanese developers of the pre-"Liberation" days. There was a bustling among the passengers as the train halted in the station sheds. Jasmine stood up with him.

"Do you know where to go?"

"Haystead briefed me on the contacts to make. I don't know how safe they will be."

She said sadly, "I won't betray you, Sam darling."

He said nothing. The train stopped. There was a huge red and gold banner above the station platform, quoting Mao: THE EAST WIND WILL PREVAIL OVER THE WEST. He heard the inevitable blare of martial music from the loudspeakers, the rattle of an orator exhorting the people to voluntary labor on public projects to "defeat the dogs of imperialist capitalism." There were steaming noodle stands and endless swarms of people, who were better dressed here than in the countryside.

Jasmine gripped his arm. "Listen."

He had already heard the whistles. There was a surge of movement among the people on the platform, a turning of heads, a rising decibel-level of noise. Durell swung down into the middle of the crowd with Jasmine. He had to fight down the feeling that he was different and alien in this tide of Oriental faces and remember he was Major Shan and looked and thought Chinese. The cause of the disturbance was a row of militiamen with fixed bayonets, working their way down the station platform. He didn't doubt that word had been telegraphed ahead to trap him here. Jasmine's grip on his arm tightened. He looked toward the food stalls and worked that way, seeking further confusion in which to lose himself; but there was no real place to hide. In a few minutes, the line of militiaman would reach them.

"Comrade Shan?" asked a mild voice.

He turned, trying not to show surprise. There was a small knot of Buddhist monks with bald pates right behind them, carrying small parcels as if they, too, had been on the train. The speaker was a small man in a gray robe —not the usual saffron of the Buddhist hierarchy—and he wore round, gold-rimmed spectacles over smiling, slanted eyes.

"I am from the Temple of Lute-Playing," the monk murmured. "Do you know it?"

"It is an historic jewel," Durell replied, dredging the contact words from his memory of the long list of signals that Haystead had given him. "It is my humble wish to visit this ancient treasure at once."

"You and the young lady—" the priest bowed and smiled at Jasmine—"must come with me. You both speak Mandarin?"

"Just myself. The lady speaks only Cantonese."

"Then let the woman be silent."

The militiamen were only a few steps away, sifting through the crowds on the platform like fishermen seining for sardines. One of them had seen Durell and was calling for his sergeant and pointing. The little Buddhist priest wrinkled his eyes behind his gold spectacles.

"We will discuss the restoration of my temple through the overflowing kindness of the People's Republic government. We will be very engrossed in our conversation. Have no fear."

The soldiers were making directly for Durell and the gray-garbed priests. There was a subtle rearrangement of the monks, so that Durell and Jasmine were screened by four or five of them, and the chief monk, who called himself Hao, talked to Durell over the sound of a wistful little folk song that now came from the propaganda speakers. A train began to pull out on the opposite track, and a tide of people who had come to see others off disturbed the militiamen's even line.

"If I seem to teach you," said Hao, "one must remember that Confucius said we must not feel ashamed to learn from the people below us. I am at your command, Major Shan. Just as the government sets up these posters, these *ta tsebaos,* in all places in order to influence the minds of the people, so must we, for Buddha's precious sake, carry on against all handicaps. Excuse me, sir."

The militia officer had halted them. Hao stepped forward and spoke in a rapid jargon of progaganda phrases. His manner, though polite and subservient, was firm, even angry. He spoke of Durell as a distinguished historian they had come to meet and honor at the temple. There was more confusion on the platform as other passengers demanded to go by. The officer was dubious and pointed again at Durell, his manner suddenly furious.

"We must walk on two legs," Hao said sharply. "This is Mao's own slogan for the Chinese people, officer! Education and labor for socialist development, is this not true?"

Hao then produced an astonishing sheaf of documents from under his gray robe and thrust them impatiently at the militiaman. His band of monks swept Durell and Jasmine through the military line before the officer could pore through even a few of the impressive sheets of sealed papers.

In a moment they were out on the city street.

There were some Russian-built and British cars waiting for them. The monks piled in, chattering and laughing like schoolboys on a holiday. Hao's face shone with sweat. He took off his glasses and smiled apologetically as they got into a car.

"That was not difficult, sir, but it could have been uncomfortable. We have only brief respite, I am sure."

"How did you know I was on that train?" Durell asked.

"We were warned," Hao said. "We have—ah—a form of radio communication."

"Who do you work for, then? Is it McFee?"

"I do not know that honorable name. I do not know the true names of any of those for whom I undertook to communicate certain data which seemed important to those who sympathize with the needs of certain elements in China. Not all of us," smiled Hao, "are Communists enchanted by the words of Chairman Mao."

"How long can you hide us?" Jasmine asked.

The little monk's eyes flicked toward her, and it seemed to Durell that he went wary. "My instructions are to forward you on toward Peking at once."

Trains rumbled across the huge double-decker Yangtze River bridge. The day was hot. The sky was a sooty ochre from the steel-mill chimneys. They passed cinemas advertising the latest Chinese musicals, swung around the famous Ming Tombs reservoir and the Great Hall of the People, then to the restored Buddhist temple that Peking had named a national monument.

"This way," Hao said hurriedly.

There were wide steps hollowed shallow by centuries of worshippers ascending into the scented gloom of the entrance hall. Red lamps glowed like dragon's eyes from their chains in the ceiling, weaving patterns of smoke against the carved timbers. On great shelves against the walls were wooden *lohans*, images of disciples in hundreds of moods. These were golden red—some as tall as twenty feet—standing, kneeling, reading, jumping; and next to them were carved chests, silk scrolls, parchments, screens depicting soldiery at the monastery, flags, and worshippers. Through the shrill intonations of the monks within came the harsh lecture of a government guide leading a group of sightseers about the national monument.

"This way," Hao said. "You must stay until dark."

"But we were seen with you at the station," Jasmine said. "Won't they come here for us? You'll be in trouble——"

"Not at all," Hao smiled.

There was a little garden enclosed by stone columns and shaded from the hot sun by wide, upturned eaves that swept gracefully from corner to corner. Hao led the way through a gate and down a dim, scented corridor lined with dragon screens and opened a heavily paneled door to reveal a small, graceful room. "Rest here," he said. His gold-rimmed glasses glinted. "An acolyte will bring refreshments. One must be patient. Do not speak too loudly."

When he left, Durell heard the click of a large, ancient key in the iron lock. He did not know if they were prisoners or guests.

Ten

THREE DAYS LATER THEY WERE IN PEKING. The pride and heart of the ancient Middle Kingdom of old China was adrift under an autumn sun with thousands of Chinese flags, with their five gold stars on a red field. It was late September, and preparations were being made for National Day. If tensions threatened to fragment the incredible vastness of the Chinese nation, no signs were visible here. The major streets, such as the Yungtingmen leading to the old Legation Quarter, the People's Heroes' Monument, the Cultural Palace, and the Forbidden City, were aswarm with banner-waving, shouting, marching Red Guard youths and working-class cadres, singing and shouting slogans in a monolithic, mindless unison that made Durell's scalp crawl. This sea of humanity in China's oldest city, built on the nucleus of famed Cambaluc, Kublai Khan's capital, was too much for a newcomer to accept easily.

Hao was still with them. At the last moment, after the one night in Wuhan, Hao managed to get government permission to come to Peking, ostensibly to pursue further restoration in the Temple of Lute-Playing.

"Our contact for the Lotus Group has—ah—vanished. He was a former monk who became a minor governmental functionary as a cultural expert on antiquities. His speciality was the Ch'ing dynasty and its architectural developments."

"What happened to him?" Durell asked.

"We do not know, Comrade Shan."

"How often do you contact Lotus?"

"We use the radio once weekly, at regular intervals. We have not been detected yet." Hao's eyes glittered behind his round spectacles, and something about him reminded Durell of McFee—perhaps his calm grayness, the sense of power behind a mild façade. Hao said, "We can use the temple quarters just outside the Tatar City, near the wall. Your—ah, wife—will have to be discreet."

Jasmine only smiled tightly at the remark. They passed the enormous new department store and went north on the busy Wangfu Tachien beyond the Capital Theater into the Tungtan district, east of the Forbidden City. There were trolleys and buses, but autos were practically nonexistent. Bicycles formed the chief mode of private transportation, filling the broad boulevards in torrents under a light, cool rain that began to fall. They had passed through a huge gate in the walls that still enclosed the teeming reaches of the Inner City. New workers' apartments, aping Russia's communal concrete blocks, had been recently built around equally new industrial complexes. Everywhere were banners, loudspeakers, the endless propaganda demands to work, to give, to volunteer for the betterment of socialism and the Chinese People's Republic.

"Here we are," Hao said.

They had turned into a less modern area off the main boulevard. The streets were narrower, the housing consisted of remnants of old Manchu tenements, bursting with people. There were small restaurants, noodle stands, mean little shops with poor quality goods, and fewer of the propaganda banners.

"This way," Hao said.

He seemed quite familiar with the area. There was a

small, closed temple, ignored by the busy people, and a small park with newly planted trees on one side of the alley they used.

"In the old days," Hao said, "before the Manchus were overthrown, this place was almost entirely populated by palace servants and temple attendants." He looked sad. "So much has been mercilessly destroyed. We Chinese are like a river of time, and part of our source of life has been wiped out."

"But your order has survived," Durell pointed out.

"We monks live only on sufferance, today. It is only a matter of time before the Interior Ministry decides we are no longer needed. The older people would resist if we were destroyed now. But in another ten years we will be gone."

Behind the closed temple was a small, walled area of crumbling brick. Hao had a key to the gate. It was growing dark, and the rain had thickened and felt colder on their thin cotton clothing. Durell recalled the gradual change in the countryside, seen from the train between the Yangtze and Yellow Rivers. Rice had given way to rolling fields of cotton that stretched to a far horizon, broken only by occasional clumps of trees or by clustered villages of mud and straw. Peking, as a metropolis, was a stark contrast to the vast rural areas they had traveled.

In the quarters that Hao led them to, it was as if they had stepped into China's early feudal ages. Dim red lanterns showed highly polished, fretwork furniture, urns, wall scrolls, a richly figured carpet. Incense coiled in the air. There were two bedrooms, separated from the brick kitchen, and Hao led Jasmine to one of them. "You must rest, dear lady. You look exhausted. Shan and I must talk."

He closed the door firmly against her protest, then clapped a hand, and an old woman with her hair skinned back in a bun, wearing white cotton, came in with fragrant tea in a fragile pot. Hao's bushy brows lifted for a moment.

"Do you trust the young woman, Shan?"

"No more than I trust you, Hao," Durell said.

The monk smiled. "Have I not helped you?"

"So far. Do you know my job?"

"You wish to find the Black House and enter it."

"Do you know where it is?"

"Yes. I am a priest of Buddha, and although in times past in my country's history there were many monasteries of fighting monks who devoted themselves to the overthrow of tyrants, I am a man of peace. The problem of entering the Black House, to reach General Chien Y-Wu, who is a prisoner there, must be solved by you and you alone."

"You know my mission, it seems."

"The Lotus Group briefed me, yes."

"And you approve?"

"One must survive. I struggle, in my own way, but my path is peace and I abhor violence."

"How safe are we here?"

"One never knows how much information L-5 may have. Certainly we monks, who have only the most grudging toleration of the State, are under constant surveillance. But this place, so far, has been kept secure."

Durell had to be content. He drank the warm, sweet tea, ate a sugared kumquat from a cloisonné tray, and listened to Hao talk of recent years and the slow organization of the Lotus apparatus, while the old Chinese woman served them steamed chicken with *hua-tiao* wine, fried shrimp paste, and then a soup of noodles, hot pastries, bitter-sweet lotus seeds in syrup, and black tea. Now and then the woman said something about Jasmine, asking if she should be fed, too. Durell nodded, and the door was unlocked and a tray taken in. The girl looked furious.

"Am I a prisoner, Sam? What's the matter? I got you on the train, I helped you here, I saved your life——!"

"Take it easy, Jasmine," he said sharply. "And speak in Chinese." She had lapsed into English, in her anger.

"I'm sorry. But Hao seems to be on our side——"

"Right now, I don't know whose side *I'm* on, to tell you the truth," Durell said. "My job is to reach Chien Y-Wu, right? You're supposed to help me. Be patient, then. Hao won't be rushed into anything."

When he closed the door, he locked her in again.

There was a small garden beyond old wooden doors that led from the temple quarters. It was surrounded by brick walls, although noises from the tenements about them provided an overtone of screeching radios, voices, a dinning of gongs. The rain had slackened, and Hao led him into the dusty darkness of the temple. They went down a flight of steps into a cellar that smelled fragrantly of ancient storage of incense and spices. There was another door, and Hao took a flashlight from under his gray robe, switched it on, and sighed with relief. "All is untouched. The L-5 would not have let this remain, if my co-religionist who has vanished had been made to talk."

He showed Durell a radio transmitter and described how the antenna was carefully concealed in the tiled eaves of the roof high above them. "We use a frequency that the L-5 monitors have not scanned as yet."

"They'll find you, sooner or later, with a mobile search team," Durell said.

The monk shrugged. "It will be as Buddha directs. In this life, one walks the path of rightness, as one sees it, but no man can divine the true will of God."

"They'll shoot you as a traitor and close every temple in the country, if you're caught."

"I have a plan for that. I will not be taken alive," the little man said quietly. "Can you use this equipment?" When Durell nodded, Hao said, "Then we will sleep for a time. Go to the girl and calm her. Your suspicions of her may or may not be right, but she must be comforted. At midnight, I will show you the way to the Black House."

In the dark bedroom, warm and glowing in the huge Chinese bed, Jasmine said: "Are you playing a Jack-and-Jill game with Hao about me, Sam?"

"I don't know what you mean."

"Showing him you don't trust me, so maybe he'll say

something about me and let you know which way the balance tips for him? You don't trust him, either, do you?"

"Hao seems all right."

"How can you make love to me when you hate me so?"

"I don't hate you, Jasmine."

"You resent McFee sending me along to spy on you."

"It's all part of the business."

She said suddenly, "But it's a rotten business."

"I've been in it a long time."

"Did you ever want to get out—to be like everybody else?" she whispered. "With a home, children, a commuter schedule?"

"Yes."

"With Deirdre Padgett?"

"Yes."

"Did you ever think that they—McFee—will never let you out of the agency?"

"I know they will never dare let me go," Durell said.

"You could always defect, of course," she whispered. "*They* would always welcome you."

He began to laugh, softly, making the bed shake in the dark room, and Jasmine cupped his face in her hands and bent over him, her body sliding like warm silk over his, her breasts firm and excited by his touch. He laughed quietly, without making much sound, and she asked him what was so funny, but he shook his head and did not answer her question.

After a time, he forced himself to sleep.

Eleven

IT TOOK EIGHT DAYS TO FIND A POSSIBLE WAY INTO the Black House. Ike Greentree had given him three weeks before the pigmentation process would begin to wear off. His contact lenses bothered him, too, and at night he had to take them out to prevent eye inflammation. Now and then he checked the subcutaneous pads of silicone in his cheeks to insure there was no slippage there. He always felt as if he were walking on the edge of a knife.

On the eighth day, he saw Tai Ma, the fat chief of L-5. Durell sat in a small restaurant, drinking Five Goats beer, and looked down the tree-lined street at the walls surrounding the stronghold where General Chien Y-Wu was secluded. He wondered how much time he had left. Chien could have talked his guts out by now, but it was impossible to know.

Durell wore cheap straw sandals and a worker's blue quilted cotton jacket and pants. He had allowed his moustache to grow longer, and his face was thinner where the silicone did not round him out. He looked gaunt and hungry.

It was plain, from the view he had from the restaurant, that Communist China's policy of encouraging visitors from sympathetic countries was up against the ancient prejudices that that had kept the old Middle Kingdom aloof from "barbarians." What few Afro-Asians, Japanese, and occasional Europeans he saw were lost in the sea of bicycles and pedestrian workers sweeping back and forth in their antlike progress through the days. A cool wind flapped the sprouting banners that proclaimed National Day, which would soon be celebrated. There were floats, groups of dancers in bright costumes, cadres of young marchers from Peking University. The clash of music, gongs, shrill singing, chanted slogans, all challenged the cool whip of the wind that fluttered the propaganda banners. Directly across from the restaurant, the building was swathed in a giant painting depicting Chinese youths fighting against monstrous, ogrelike imperialists. Portraits of Chairman Mao grew bigger and brighter each day. Little ceramic busts of China's aging leader were peddled from stands at almost every street corner. The *ta tsebaos*—"big character news"—were plastered on every available wall, giving production figures and the names of model workers and students.

The waiter in the restaurant offered a cup of weak

green tea. Durell shook his head, put down a five yuan note, and walked out into the cool wind. Down the tree-lined street the looming wall of the Black House resisted him for the eighth day. He bought a *People's Daily* and walked past the one gate in the high compound barrier, and it was then that he saw Tai Ma Cho.

The black Zis limousine swept in from the street and almost brushed his leg as it ignored pedestrians and cy-clists. Durell jumped back just in time. The great brass-bound gate swung open and he glimpsed a garden, a shell walk, thick shrubbery, and a black-painted wooden pal-ace structure that might have been built in China's Mid-dle Ages. The area covered several city blocks, and the guarded, lighted walls had blocked his every effort to gain entry for the past week.

The fat Tai Ma looked straight ahead as his Zis carried him into the forbidden area. The intelligence chief of L-5 looked grim, even petulant; his jowls sagged and his lower lip was angry. Durell did not think the fat man had seen him.

He went back to the restaurant where he could watch the gate. The waiter, whom he had told he was on sick leave from his factory, brought him tea and rice. He waited an hour, and Tai Ma did not come out. Dusk was falling. The chanting parades and practicing singers went on and on, in preparation for their massed celebrations. When it was altogether dark, and the fat man had not reappeared, he got up and walked back to the apartment behind the temple.

Jasmine looked pale and distant. "No luck?"

"I saw Tai Ma go in, finally. But not out."

"Hao has to make a radio report tonight, and he says he should go back to Wuhan tomorrow." Suddenly the Chinese girl sank to her knees before him. "Sam, don't keep me a prisoner here. Please let me help you!"

"All right," he said.

She looked up with a start. "You'll trust me now? Just tell me what to do. I'll do anything. I sit here day after day while you're out, and I'm sick with fear that someone will spot you and turn you in."

"Maybe I should let them. It may be the only way to get into the Black House."

"But you wouldn't live a day!" she protested. "You know how L-5 wants to get you. Oh, Sam—Sam, I want——"

"When Hao returns, send him in to me."

He stretched out on the bed and slept. He had long ago learned to be patient in his business; but much of the work was slow and tedious, the painful gathering of information and resources. As a boy in the Louisiana bayous, he had often gone hunting with his grandfather, and the old gentleman had taught him how to wait for his quarry, to hold back until the precise moment when the chance for success was at an optimum. But this was different. He felt that this waiting was being forced upon him, and that he was playing the enemy's game by the delay, although he could not yet identify the enemy, or even know the game he was playing. His objective was to rescue or silence the defecting General Chien. But he could not reach the man, or see any way to do so; and no matter which way he turned, he was up against the blank walls of the Black House. To try to scale them at night would be suicidal. To give himself up, just to gain entry, was equally foolish. The Black House people comprised the most efficient espionage operation in China—perhaps in all the world.

But now he might have Tai Ma.

It was almost midnight when Hao appeared. The monk was dubious when Durell described his plan.

"Yes, I know where Tai Ma lives," Hao said. "But it is as impossible to reach him there as in the Black House."

"It must be done," Durell said.

"Yes, I agree to that now." Hao meditated a moment. "Buddha, in his wisdom, made man intelligent—less strong than many animals, but with a mind made to conquer without the use of fangs or talons." He paused. "We must use the girl."

"Jasmine? Yes, if we can."

Hao smiled. "Tai Ma likes beautiful women."

They called in Jasmine and told her what to do. Her face changed subtly, and Durell knew she was recalling her early years in San Francisco when she was a child sold to an elderly merchant, followed by her abduction to Singapore where she was forced to entertain as a prostitute. He knew she had hoped that was all behind her, and he watched her draw a deep breath; he could not read beyond the pain that clouded her dark, almond eyes.

"You don't have to do it, Jasmine," he said.

"I will. I want to." She smiled grimly. "It's my one qualification, isn't it?"

"Don't feel that way. In this business——"

"I don't mind," she interrupted. "I'm not good for much else, in your eyes, it seems."

He didn't argue about it. They discussed the problem, then Hao made some phone calls and said they would have to wait until dawn. Jasmine shut the bedroom door firmly behind her.

It actually took two more days to set it up, and another day for Jasmine to make contact with Tai Ma. Hao produced all the papers needed; the little monk's resources were remarkable. Peking at one time had had more "Mist and Flower Maidens" than any other Chinese city, but the Communist regime had removed these women from the streets. Still, the age-old trade flourished secretly. Jasmine was moved into the Chien Men, the Front Gate Hotel, a sprawling modern structure with quiet service and poor food. Hao got her a costume of a long, black Chinese-style dress, several woolen sweaters, and an elaborate opera costume with an enormous headdress studded with pearls, representing an Emperor's concubine.

Durell helped her get established. It was an easy walk from the hotel to the nearby Temple of Heaven, with its triple, blue-tiled roofs above vermilion walls. Dark green cypress trees surrounded the shrine. Under the arch of the Front Gate, the wide street was crowded with jingling bicycles, modern trolley buses, and ancient handcarts pushed by women. From Jasmine's hotel window, they could see the Square of the Gate of Heavenly Peace, where much of National Day's festivities would take place. Most of the buildings were shrouded in wrappings of banners. In the other direction, toward Changan Boulevard, above the clusters of lamp standards and Edwardian buildings around the rose-pink walls and golden roofs of the Forbidden City, the spire of the white Buddhist dagoba in Peihai Park loomed against a sapphire, autumn sky. Directly under the hotel room was a huge banner reading, LONG LIVE THE PEOPLE'S REPUBLIC OF CHINA—LONG LIVE THE UNITY OF THE NATIONS OF THE WORLD.

Jasmine was unimpressed as Durell helped to stow her luggage. "I wish it were all true," she said quietly.

"What?"

"All this progress. It's good, isn't it, Sam? I mean, those people lived in hovels, in such wretched poverty——"

"Yes."

The inevitable loudspeaker in the room gave out with several falsetto screeches from recordings of the Peking Opera. Jasmine went on, "The railroad station here, when we arrived, the Beijing Zhan? And all the people who use it, who never left their mud huts and villages in their lifetimes. It's a beautiful building, don't you think?"

"If you like neo-Empire in today's Chinese style," he said.

He, too, had been impressed with the station, its enormous façade of creamy stone, the Chinese-style roof and turrets, the vast foyer of polished marble and potted plants, the cleaning women in their hygienic gauze masks.

"How long must I be here?" Jasmine asked. Her voice was plaintive. "I don't like being away from you, Sam."

"Tai Ma comes into this restaurant every day. He hands reports to subordinates then," Durell said. "And Hao says he has a weakness for tall Chinese women, beautiful women."

"Am I beautiful, Sam?"

"You are."

"But suppose I have to—have to——?"

"We all do what we must."

Her dark eyes were wounded and glistening. Durell turned up the public loudspeaker in the hotel room. The screeching operatic aria had ended, and now martial music blared in the room. Jasmine winced. He said, "I've fanned the place and can't find any bugs; but you know what electronic eavesdropping is like. A transmitter could be anywhere."

"Sam, don't you care at all what may happen to me?"

"I do," he said. "You know that. But you were briefed on these risks when you took on the job. If you want, you can go back to Hao and wait for me to do the job without you."

"Could you?"

"I doubt it."

She smiled tearfully. "I'll manage Tai Ma, don't worry. Give me a couple of days for it, that's all."

He looked at his Chinese face in the mirror. According to Ike Greentree, he'd had three weeks in which to finish this mission before he started to look less Chinese. More than half that time was already gone now.

"Just get Tai Ma up here soon, Jasmine," he said.

He never quite knew how she managed it. He could not remain in the Chien Men Hotel all the time, because of the industrious cleaning women who seemed obsessed with the diligent performance of their job. At night he waited until Jasmine came in alone, and then he would eat with her and talk of her work with the Canton Opera for the benefit, he was sure, of eavesdropping microphones in the room. Finally, on the second day, he found one in a simple bouquet of flowers. It was a marvel of ingenuity, a tiny transmitter smaller than a hazel nut. It probably broadcast on voice impulses to tape recorders in the security office of the big hotel. He left it where it was.

Hao's information on Tai Ma proved correct. The fat L-5 chief was a regular patron of the hotel restaurant, and he always had an artist, dancer, or singer with him. Peking was crowded to the bursting point with the delegations and celebrants for National Day, and Tai Ma seemed to have his pick of the finest beauties in China.

On the third night of his watch in the hotel room, Jasmine came up later than usual. He lay on her bed in the semi-gloom broken only by the flashing neon light of newly erected signs in the boulevard below. He drank beer quietly, wishing for a cup of Louisiana coffee laced with bourbon. He was beginning to feel uneasy about her delayed return when he heard her signal at the door.

He rolled silently off the bed, flattened on the floor in the dark shadow under the windowsill. The gaudy signs on the boulevard flickered on and off, splashing the sterile, communal hotel furniture with bright waves of alternating color. He heard Jasmine's key and the murmur of her voice, speaking Cantonese, and then he moved like a shadow through a wave of red and saffron color into the closet. Her perfume engulfed him.

There was a little foyer and sitting room—it was one of the Chien Men's best suites, thanks to Hao's mysterious influence—and he saw the light go on and heard Tai Ma's thick voice, heavy with liquor and food, gasping a little as he replied to Jasmine's California-accented Chinese.

"My dear Comrade, I must see this costume you will use with the Cantonese troupe tomorrow. The Chairman and the Committee will surely be enraptured by your performance."

"In a moment, Comrade Tai," she replied. "Please wait and be comfortable."

"I've brought the wine. I shall amuse myself."

In the closet where Durell stood was the elaborate headdress and embroidered operatic costume that Hao had procured for Jasmine. She slid the door open. He stood partly in the shadow as the light from the sitting room leaped across the wide bed. Jasmine's eyes were almost level with his. They were wide, but expressionless, and her rich mouth was taut. Her long black hair had been swept up in an elaborate coiffure, with pearled combs of silver and jade. It had been necessary to make her stand out against the usual Communist drabness in order to attract Tai Ma's lustful eye.

He signaled silently to Jasmine to delay returning to

the other room; she nodded, pretending to be engrossed in the costume Tai Ma wanted to see. From the closet, he glimpsed the fat man pacing back and forth. The Chinese had a small, anticipatory smile on his moustached mouth. Durell remembered the power in that deceptive, flabby-looking body. He had almost succumbed to the huge man back there in the village railroad station; but this time he hoped to have the advantage of surprise.

"Comrade?" Tai Ma called, after a moment.

"Come in here," Jasmine replied, as if absently.

The man's shadow bulked enormously in the doorway. His footsteps were soundless; his eyes were fixed on Jasmine, who moved away from the closet with the elaborate headdress fixed to her gleaming black hair. Tai Ma's eyes followed, slitted and glistening, but only after he had scanned the bed and the window. For one instant he turned his back to the closet.

Durell had chosen his knife, rather than the gun he had carried on the air-drop. He moved in one silent stride, whipped his left arm about the great pumpkin bulge of the man's chest, and made a shallow slitting cut across Tai's throat with the razor-sharp blade. Blood spouted. The fat Chinese sucked in his breath with a great, shuddering sound.

"One move," Durell whispered, "and it goes deeper."

"Shan?"

"Yes."

"I am bleeding. Am I dying?"

"Not yet."

"I did not think you would cut me."

"Be silent. Don't move."

Blood ran down the man's fat throat. A quarter of an inch more, and the esophagus would have been cut—and nothing could have saved Tai. The man shuddered as Durell pushed him toward the bed. Durell glanced at Jasmine, who stood frozen, her face white. "Get him a towel. Wipe up the mess."

"I thought——" she began haltingly.

"I haven't killed him. It's just to let him know I mean what I'm going to say."

Durell patted the man's capacious pockets and found a revolver, a small cyanide-pellet air dart, a wallet of papers, money, and brass coins. He tossed the aggregation onto a chair across the room and told Jasmine, "Don't touch any of that."

She had a wet towel. "I won't."

"Clean him up. Quickly. Tai Ma, lie down on the bed, on your back, arms wide, hands over the sides. Look up at the ceiling and don't move your head. Understand?"

The Chinese whispered, "You did not have to cut me, Shan. I was expecting you."

"Indeed?"

"I was simply wondering what took you so long."

Twelve

TAI MA DID EXACTLY AS HE WAS TOLD. THERE HAD been no alarm. Durell turned up the propaganda speaker to a louder volume, and martial music shook the suite. He decided that a complaint from the management was inevitable, but it would take a few minutes for that, and by then he should have what he wanted out of the fat man.

"You were really expecting me, Tai Ma?" he asked.

"I have studied your files carefully, Major Shan. I do not take your capacities lightly."

"Why are we enemies, then? Why were you waiting to kill me when I returned to China last week?"

The fat man stared at the ceiling. Jasmine had staunched the flow of blood from his throat. "I had orders. You were listed as a traitor, a defector."

"Why? On what evidence?"

"I do not question L-5 orders. One cannot do that. We live to obey and do our duty, Comrade."

"I am not a traitor," Durell said. "I need your help."

"Impossible. I reserve judgment."

"Would you rather die?"

Tai Ma was silent, thinking it over. His slashed throat convinced him, as Durell had hoped it would. "What do you want of me? I knew this young lady was not what she said she was. I knew this was a trap. I walked into it willingly. Modesty is not my best trait. I felt I could handle you. I did not think—I did not expect your violence, Shan."

"I am desperate," Durell said simply.

"Yes, but you cannot win."

"I think I can. What I must do is for the safety and peace of all of us—to defeat the Six Sentinels. You know about them; you mentioned them at the railroad station. I am not an agent of the Six Sentinels."

"You are working for them, whether you know it or not. The Americans have purchased your loyalty," Tai Ma said thinly. "What am I to believe?" His chest still heaved with his rapid breathing. For an instant, as Durell's knife sliced across his throat, he had thought himself a dead man. "What do you want me to do?"

"You must get me safely into the Black House."

"Why?"

"I must talk to the KMT defector, Chien Y-Wu."

Tai Ma was silent. His round moon face stared at the ceiling. The martial music thumped and rang in the hotel bedroom. Durell glanced at Jasmine. She had not moved.

"Can it be done?" Durell asked.

"To talk to that pig, Chien? No."

"It must be done."

"You will be killed, Shan. You walk into my hands like a fly into a spider's web. Are you mad?"

"Merely desperate, as I told you. I've watched your routine. We'll go together. The girl remains here, so it will be just you and I. If you make one wrong move, you die. At once. Do you believe me?"

"I do. You are clever—and quite mad."

Durell drew a long breath. "You live only until you make a mistake. Jasmine, turn down the loudspeaker. We will be silent until daybreak. Then we go to the Black House."

National Day in Peking had changed the metropolis into one huge carnival. The city glowed with splendor among its ancient palaces. In the vast area of the Imperial Quarter, among the wide courtyards, Throne Halls, marble steps and terraces, there was a vista of multiple roofs, shining with blue and amber and turquoise tiles. The wide avenues swarmed with holiday-minded people. An old man in a park was teaching shadow-boxing to youngsters, and plump button-eyed babies were gathered in kindergarten pedicabs, being taken to special stands set aside for them. Flags, banners, and lanterns were festooned everywhere. Today there were few of the old women pushing handcarts of bricks or dung. Seeing the multitudes, as Tai Ma's official limousine pushed slowly through the crowds, it was easy for Durell to believe that one out of every five people on earth was Chinese.

The festive air made things easier. Today, Premier Chou En-lai, Madame Huang, and Mao himself would appear in the vast audience square, on the reviewing stand that would be passed by parades of singers, dancers, workers, militia, tanks, artillery, and the new rocket launchers, besides symbolic representations of the New China's hydrogen bomb. The talk would be about peace, the exhibits would be for war. China was the center of the world, resurgent, powerful; all other nations, by divine law, were subservient to Peking; it was simply that they were like rebellious children, not recognizing ancient authority.

The limousine slowly circled the Temple of Heaven, in its fine park, with its huge marble altar at which the emperors once prayed at the summer soltice. Not far away was the Temple of Confucius, dating back to the Chou dynasty. Companies of troops rested here, waiting under their banners and flags for a place in the coming parade.

"You have chosen the day wisely," Tai Ma murmured.

"It's as good a day as any to die in—if you make a mistake," Durell returned.

The big limousine rolled smoothly along devious routes to avoid the massed marchers. Rain fell in a sudden shower, then eased into a dull drizzle. The sky was leaden. Tai Ma touched the muffler he wore to conceal the knife wound across his throat; his round face shone with sweat.

"May I ask how much you have been paid to do this by the enemy, Comrade Major Shan?" he asked softly.

"I have been paid nothing. What I do is for my nation, my duty only, against traitors at home and abroad, and against those warmongers who would kill millions, rather than have their political ambitions frustrated."

"We have the same goals, then. Must we be enemies?"

"You tried to kill me when we first met, remember?"

"Perhaps L-5 was misinformed. It is possible. Even under our glorious Communist State, we are not infallible, eh?"

Durell kept his hand on the gun in his pocket. All that he said could be monitored, somewhere. He didn't know if the faceless, anonymous chauffeur beyond the glass partition could overhear them or not. His nerves tightened as the car made a sudden left turn, then a right. The Black House loomed ahead through the lightly falling rain. The boulevard had been cordoned off, and there was no traffic or pedestrians in sight. The gates showed through the windshield, over the driver's shoulder.

"Do not worry, Comrade Major," Tai Ma said. "We dislike marching crowds past our headquarters. Simply a security measure, even on this day of glorious celebration."

The guards saluted, their automatic weapons held at the ready. A noncom came up in his peaked hat and quilted uniform and spoke to the chauffeur, then glanced in at Tai Ma, nodded, and waved the Zis inside.

They entered another world.

Beyond the high walls that shut off the tree-lined avenue, the compound was one of palatial elegance in the old Imperial palace style. The limousine rolled silently along a curving driveway between black-tiled, curved roofs, jewellike gardens, and tiny lacquered bridges over ponds that reflected autumn tree branches and stone lanterns like so many giant gems.

Tai Ma chuckled. "You look surprised, Shan. This was once the home of the Emperor Ch'ung's favorite concubine, and——"

"Do you forget, Tai Ma, that I have worked out of this center for some years?" Durell asked coldly.

"Ah, yes. Forgive me, but you seemed so interested. And there have been some changes here, true?" Tai Ma asked.

Durell took a chance. "I notice none, as yet."

"You are right. None, outwardly. But do you remember our research on the many miles of tunnels that once connected this palace with the Imperial complex? It was like discovering another world used by the Emperors to avoid being too closely observed by the populace as they went about their private affairs. Most fascinating—and useful to us, you may be sure."

"Just take me to General Chien as quickly as possible."

"Yes, I know your temper better now." The fat man seemed more cheerful now that they were within the walls of the Black House. "I must check in first, of course."

"Skip it," Durell said shortly. "I haven't much time."

"Unfortunately, the chauffeur has orders to ignore any commands I may give that are not part of the established security schedule. I value my life, comrade, as must be obvious to you, and I suggest we do not cause any alarms."

The car stopped before the main building. Durell saw no choice but to accept Tai Ma's word for what was necessary. A uniformed soldier opened the car doors. Tai Ma grunted and squeezed out, and Durell followed close behind. There was no sign here of the national celebration going on all through Peking today. Everything was swift, cold efficiency. Tags were pinned on the fat man and Durell after Tai Ma briefly identified and vouched for Durell's presence. There was no reaction from the guards, and Durell enjoyed a brief respite from his tension.

"This way," Tai Ma said. "To my humble little office."

The building had been kept as intact as possible in the old architectural style. There were enough treasures in tapestries, painted screens, porcelains, and fine furniture to stock a modest museum, Durell reflected. The Black House did well for itself. The incongruity of trim young Chinese typists in blue smocks, the sound of bells from teletype machines, did not bother him. Tai Ma moved swiftly, for all his ponderous bulk, through what had been a huge Imperial reception hall, with red-painted timbered ceilings, between the rows of young women stenographers, then on across a small covered court and into a maze of cubby-like offices. Tea was being served. The hot fragrance was infinitely superior to that served to the masses on the trains and in public restaurants.

Tai Ma sniffed appreciatively. "It is my routine to ring at once for tea, you understand."

"Forget it, this time," Durell ordered. "I'm getting nervous. Have you forgotten my gun? You won't be easy to miss."

"But you will never get out of here alive, now."

"Then neither will you. Take me to Chien."

"Are you so impatient to silence him? I wonder if you have any personal reasons. Chien is a notorious womanizer. Did he by any chance steal a woman from you?"

"Wrong track, Tai. I'll kill Chien, yes, but only if it's necessary—even though a traitor, of any kind, even from the enemy side, is a loathsome creature."

"I agree. But I remind you that General Chien Y-Wu is a voluntary defector to our cause, in disgrace with the imperialist KMT on Taiwan. He came to us of his own free will. You know the details, eh? A weak man, but most knowledgeable in the details of American electronic espionage equipment and information-gathering methods. His data will be invaluable."

"Hasn't he talked much yet?"

Tai Ma blandly stroked his moustache. "We have treated him kindly so far, indulging his vices. We suspect that he has given us only a small portion of the information he can be made to yield. Being soft, he thinks he can blackmail us for the luxuries, the food and women, he has always craved. A disgusting creature, my dear Shan, typical of Western decadence. But our own patience has run out. Today he will be shown the fine print in his contract with us. We don't doubt that a sudden and shocking change in his circumstances will now make him babble like a spring brook." Tai Ma looked bleak. "If you renounce this insane mission to silence him, it will be to your credit. I do not know what dangerous conspiracy you have become involved in, but much may be forgiven if you allow our glorious People's Republic to reap the benefit of so many months of patience with this revolting and disgusting creature."

"When did you intend to put pressure on him?"

"Today, comrade. It was on our agenda for some time, before you returned and began to interfere."

Durell thought for a moment. He stood tall and ominous in Tai Ma's elegant little office. His borrowed Chinese face was immobile. He heard several gongs echo softly through the antique building, and he was aware of the fat man's intense scrutiny of his features, as a tiny flicker of puzzlement came and went in the other's shrewd eyes. It passed quickly. At last Durell said, "I'll indulge you for a bit. Let's go to him now."

They went out into the light falling dawn rain. Durell began to wonder if his luck would hold; he wasn't even sure if it was luck that had brought him this far. Until now, he had been moved only as a pawn in a deadly conspiratorial chess game, the outlines of which he could only glimpse. Soon it would be time to make his own move and break the pattern of the game; it was his only chance of survival. The unexpected, the apparently illogical move, might get him safely out of it. He had to make the move soon—Tai Ma had recovered too much confidence—but it must not really be illogical, from his viewpoint. Back in his boyhood days in Louisiana, his Grandpa Jonathan had played chess and poker with him in this manner, teaching him to confound his opponents with the unexpected. In all his years at K Section, he had not forgotten these lessons, although his behavior had often been deplored by the strategists at No. 20 Annapolis Street in Washington. But he had survived. He hoped to survive again.

The Black House compound was more complex than it appeared. There were hidden and unexpected buildings behind these walls, large and small; a maze of courts, gemlike little temples and pavilions, all with the familiar black-tiled Chinese roofs. They were halted at a gate in a low wall, guarded by Manchurian soldiers. The delay was brief. Then they found themselves in an area of small, elegant pavilions near a tall pagoda. Two more burly Manchurians, in winter uniforms, were obviously waiting for Tai Ma.

"Is everything ready?" the fat man asked cheerfully.

"He has had his usual meal, and has eaten and drunk like a pig and sent for the two women he enjoyed recently." The Manchurian barked his report with disgust. Then he grinned, showing a gap in his front teeth. "It has been difficult to pamper the running dog of an imperialist for so many weeks."

"His good time has ended, you may be sure. He was a fool not to cooperate, eh? Come. Major Shan will be with us to observe our new methods. They will prove instructive."

The man's slanted eyes considered Durell. "Very good. Are you armed, Comrade Major?"

Durell did not hesitate. "Yes, with Comrade Tai's permission——"

There was a brief pause, a momentary silence that told him that this time he had said the wrong thing. Evidently it was against rules to carry weapons here. But it couldn't be helped now. He kept his hand on the gun in his pocket. The pause ended as the burly Manchurian shrugged, and Durell could only hope for the best. They went on.

The small house with its red columns and upturned black eaves had once been a summer pavilion for the Emperor's concubine. Heavy doors had been added recently, with good-luck tiger dragons over the portal. A man's shrill laughter echoed from within as one of the Manchurians unlocked the brass-bound door. They

stepped into perfumed shadows, on a rich carpet over
teak plank flooring. No luxury had been spared in the
furnishings. Ruby eyes in a grotesque dragon lamp glared
at them from its brass face, and somewhere a gong
sounded softly. A white-jacketed servant hurried to them,
bowed, nodded to the Manchurians, and said, "All is as
usual, Comrades."

"It is the last day of his summer," Tai Ma pronounced.
"He does not suspect?"

"He knows nothing, Comrade."

Tai Ma grunted. "So much the better."

There was a moment when one of the Manchurians
tried unobtrusively to get between Durell and Tai. Durell
moved closer to the fat man, the gun nudging Tai's broad
back. The security chief negligently waved the burly
guard aside.

"Come, Shan. It will be amusing."

They were led into an inner room, with fretwork sliding panels that opened on an exquisite view of a tiled
court. It was warm here, but Durell could not locate the
source of heat. His attention was fixed on General Chien
Y-Wu—the apparent object of his assignment—and he
felt immediate disgust.

The odor of heavy, rich food permeated the air, sour-
ing the incense that curled from a heavy bronze brazier.
Platters and trays were scattered everywhere. The smell
of rancid wine did not help. There were couches with tiger's-paw legs, massed with cushions, and a massive gilt
mirror of Victorian design, perhaps from the reign of the
last Dowager Empress of the Manchus. As they paused in
the entrance, the mirror reflected the sprawling, nude
figure of a middle-aged Chinese, thin in the shoulders and
chest, pot-bellied, with a narrow black moustache and
thinning hair. He was on his back—what could be seen of
him—and was half smothered by the equally nude, agile
bodies of two Chinese girls, very young, whose giggles
were stifled by the rolling smooth flesh. It was hard to tell
whose limbs belonged to which of the trio. Although it
was now broad daylight on this rainy day, the big room
was further lighted by lanterns—evidently ex-General

Chien liked to define what he was doing—and for a moment the tableau might have been out of the wildest blue movie of pre-Castro Havana days, Durell thought grimly.

There was a squawking of Chinese operatic music from an incongruously modern hi-fi in one corner of the room. Gongs clashed, samisens screeched, and a man's falsetto went up and down the atonal scales of the Peking aria.

Tai Ma lifted a finger. One of the Manchurians crossed the room and kicked the stero player. It crashed into sudden silence. There was a paralysis among the indulgent trio playing their sex game on the couch, and for a moment they were frozen in a ridiculous pose. Then one of the girls screamed, her red painted mouth wide and round. It was choked off as the second burly Manchurian tore her free of the tangle of sweaty limbs. She sprawled on the floor and whimpered, pushing back her tangled black hair. The second girl slid quickly off the Chinese man and huddled against the wall as if she wished she could vanish through it. She evidently recognized the meaning of the Manchurians, and her eyes went wide with horror.

"We only obeyed orders," she whimpered.

"Get out!" Tai Ma said.

Both naked girls scuttled from the room. Chien Y-Wu was left alone and defenseless on the tumbled couch.

"Sit up General," Tai Mai said flatly. "You look stupid, you know."

The defector stuttered. "How dare—it is not expected —you promised not to interfere while I did your work——"

"We know your work. We have indulged you long enough."

"I need—I need my glasses."

One of the Manchurians threw a black-rimmed pair of glasses at the naked, scrawny figure. Chien, Durell thought, was pathetic in some respects. He tried to bluster, but his hands trembled as he adjusted the glasses on his saddle nose. He was covered with sweat and lipstick on his pot-belly, and he shivered as he swung his chicken legs over the edge of the couch.

"We made a bargain, Tai. I have kept my end of it. Perhaps I—perhaps I asked for too much. I tried not to be a nuisance, but I have certain tastes. It hurt no one, did it? I consider your intrusion here an outrage——"

"Stand up," Tai Ma said.

"I have been working on the lastest Lotus VII device —electronic listening pick up with a range over one hundred miles—a really remarkable achievement of the Americans——"

One of the Manchurians hauled Chien bodily off the couch and hurled him, naked, across the room. His head collided with the bronze incense brazier and toppled it over with a crash. Blood trickled from the prisoner's confused face. Only now, as reality dawned, did true terror gleam in those soft eyes.

"I told you to stand up," Tai Ma repeated. "You seem to have forgotten our true relationship."

"We—we made a bargain——"

"You did not read all of the contract, I think."

"I don't understand. You promised certain accommodations, certain—ah—comforts. In return, I've been making schematic drawings, writing descriptions of electronic equipment you have been so eager to have——"

"It has taken you months, Chien Y-Wu."

"But it has been difficult to reconstruct!"

"We think," Tai Ma said smoothly, "that your habits of living have slowed up your memory processes on the data you promised. We regret the present necessity. We feel it is time to use other methods with you. So you will now come with us."

"But—" The KMT renegade looked frantically from one to the other. His eyes slid to Durell, locked with his gaze for a blank moment, then lowered to consider his nakedness. "I will get my clothes," he whispered.

"You will come as you are," Tai Ma said.

"But my rank—I have a certain dignity——"

"You were not very dignified when we entered."

Without warning, the nearest Manchurian slammed a fist into Chien's throat. Chien's head snapped, his glasses flew off his snub nose, and he fell to his hands and feet.

Tai Ma put a small but ponderous foot on the glasses and ground them to bits. Chien whimpered. The cut on his head bled on the rich carpet. Tai Ma nodded to the guards, who hauled the naked figure upright, and shoved him from the room. Durell, standing a little aside, followed the grim procession.

They did not go far. Chien's naked feet dragged on the stone pavilion floor and began to bleed. Durell kept his hand ready on the gun in his pocket; his hand was sweating. Beyond the pavilion was a small stone structure, like the ornate top of a well, heavily carved with Chinese astrological signs. The first Manchurian opened a door in the octagonal panels with a heavy iron key. Steps descended in a tight spiral under the Black House compound. It was raining harder, and the wind was cold. Chien Y-Wu shivered, his thin body already dirty and partly bloody. His eyes, blind without his glasses, turned to Durell.

"Sir, I have tried to show my good faith——"

The Manchurian hit him in the mouth, and a tooth went flying amid a small spray of blood. Chien fell into the doorway. The second guard picked him up and carried him down the steps. Tai Ma looked at Durell.

"The tunnels," he said. "A treasure trove."

"After you," Durell said. "Will he talk?"

"He will talk or die. Which do you prefer?"

"I'll indulge you for a short time," Durell said.

"If I called for help now, Shan, you would be a dead man in moments. Don't you realize that?"

"You would be the first to go."

"Perhaps not. I may be generous with you, Shan. If Chien talks, perhaps you will talk, too. We are anxious to learn all that you discovered about the American plot known as the Six Sentinels. We feel that our national existence may depend on what you have learned."

"We might make a bargain," Durell admitted.

Tai Ma nodded and intoned, "The reasonable man is a shining light under the Eye of Heaven. A man who uses his mind is not a beast of the field or a creature of the sea; he is touched with the divine."

"That hardly sounds like good Socialist doctrine."

"It is Liao Ti's philosophy. Sixth century. His poetry is exquisite."

"Not in line with Communist sentiments, however?"

"Come. You shall see some interesting things."

They went down into the earth under the Black House. Dim, utilitarian light bulbs had been strung on open wires from the cunningly fitted masonry of the stairs. Durell heard the clang of iron somewhere, as if a door had been slammed shut. It was followed by a thin, ululating scream that seemed to come from a considerable distance. Chien halted and shuddered and was pushed ahead roughly, and again fell to his hands and knees.

Tai Ma growled, "You have been living a soft life of utter decadence. It is time you faced the realities of your situation, General."

"I have done my best," the KMT man whispered. "Please, I can't see—my glasses—why did you break them?"

"You will not need them again," Tai Ma said ominously.

The tunnels led into a long-forgotten underworld. Ancient emperors of China, either through an overly acute sense of their divinity or through fear of assassins, came and went through this underground maze from the Forbidden City and the Imperial Palaces for private meetings either with concubines, statesmen, or priests. Durell had once heard that the tunnels had extended for over two hundred miles.

Whatever the past use of the labyrinth, the Black House personnel had handily turned this section under Peking's busy boulevards into a private torture house, unsuspected by anyone outside of L-5. The tunnels were solidly built, lined with cunningly joined stone, with a curved overhead that was dry and clean. Other sections might be dilapidated or caved in by floods, but this area under the Black House had been restored to a top condition. There were rows of cells behind iron doors, a whisper of air-conditioning in the shafts, and an occasional groan from anonymous victims of the glorious People's

Republic. It was a charnel house, a butcher's emporium, a dark world devoted to the infinitely exquisite tortures of China's history.

Apparently Chien Y-Wu recognized it as such and tried to drag back, struggling feebly in the arms of his burly guards.

"No, please——" he breathed. "Not here! I've given you drawings, blueprints, I haven't finished the last one——"

"It was promised two weeks ago," Tai Ma said.

The wretch was flung into a bare stone room off the main underground corridor. There was a desk, a naked light, a straw pallet in one corner. The naked Chinese shivered under the raw light. One of the Manchurians went out and returned at once with a long rack of what looked like surgical instruments—but they were of black iron, with suspicious-looking stains on the ends of skewers, knives, and pincers. Chien Y-Wu blanched and shrank back against the cold stone wall.

"W-what do you want of me?" He was in a state of total shock. "I'll tell you all you need to know. I beg of you, don't hurt me. You treated me so well——"

"And you made a fool of me," Tai Ma said flatly. "You had wine and women, every luxury your depraved mind could imagine. Was I cruel to you then? Now you see the other side of the coin."

"I cannot stand pain——"

"We shall see how much you can take, General."

Durell leaned against the stone wall. The Manchurians no longer paid attention to him. He saw now that their jobs were those of torturers for the State. Tai Ma settled with a grunt behind his desk. All his attention was also focused on the trembling, pot-bellied victim. Durell tried to feel sympathy for the pathetic man, but it was difficult. This craven object of his mission, for whom his own life might be forfeited, had brought him to this place, and he doubted now that he would ever escape alive. His face was hard as he observed the torture preparations in the cell, and he said quietly, "What do you wish to learn from this man, Comrade Tai?"

"First, we administer a lesson. The glorious Socialist State is not to be trifled with. Our goals are above mean and limited individuals. So we will teach our guest some of our good Socialist tenets. If he lives, he will then divulge all he has so carefully withheld from us."

"But he came to you willingly."

"We do not know if he is an honest defector. I think he was sent here deliberately. If so, he has been playing a much deeper game with me than it appears."

"Who would send him?" Durell asked. "His record shows him to be weak, self-indulgent, a coward. What can you believe from a man like this?"

"A man always speaks the truth under pain."

"Not always."

"You have not, perhaps, seen my methods, Shan."

It was not easy to stand in silence while Chien was subjected to preliminary "questioning." However effective ancient Chinese torture methods might have been, Tai Ma had added modern psychiatric trimmings dredged from a twisted mind. A surgical table was brought in. No threats were made. Everything was done in cold, efficient silence. At first, Chien tried to endure what was done to his body, but slowly, inevitably, horror overwhelmed him.

His first scream was ear-shattering.

It went on and on, wrenched from his thin chest with astonishing power. Tai Ma lifted a finger and one of the torturers deftly gave the victim an injection. The screams slowly bubbled away. Chien began to sigh and weep.

"I am not a man now," he whispered. "Let me go, I beg of you. I can finish the schematic sketches you want. I can do it today. But if you hurt my hands too——"

Tai folded his fingers under his chin, his elbows resting on the desk. "Who sent you here, dog?"

"I—I was never certain—of the ultimate command——"

"But it was not your idea? You were not the one who thought of your defection?"

"No, no. I was forced to. I was accused of taking military funds—my tastes in living, you see——"

"Yes, we know them well. Tell us who sent you, then."

"A wizard, a monster," Chien gasped. "A man devoted in his evil soul only to the use of nuclear weapons to impose an American peace on the whole world. I could not agree. China, Socialist or not, is my native land. I could not accept the deaths of hundreds of millions, through the plots of the Sentinels."

"Ah," said Tai Ma. "The Six Sentinels?"

Chien's ribbed chest rose and fell in rapid spasms. Saliva drooled from his slack mouth.

Durell said, "Send your two men out."

"I cannot do so," Tai Ma said quickly.

"I command here," Durell said. "Chien is mine. What he now has to say must be kept in top security." He moved behind the fat man at the desk. "Do you understand?"

Tai Ma sighed. "I thought we agreed——"

"Agreements are made to be broken, Comrade Tai."

The two Manchurians looked at Durell with gleaming eyes. Their weapons had been put aside for their preliminary work on Chien's bloody body. The KMT man looked as if he were in utter shock, after being dragged from total luxury to deepest degradation. The nearest Manchurian, however, had a pair of heavy tongs in his fist, and how he lifted them in a slight movement. The heavy iron door of the cell was closed. Durell drew his gun.

"Drop it," he snapped.

The torturers hesitated. Between them, on the table, Chien groaned and writhed. His loins were bloody from the brief attentions he had already received. He did not look like a man who had long to live.

Tai Ma sighed. "Do as Major Shan says, Comrades."

The Manchurian dropped the iron tongs and stepped back. There was another, smaller door in the cell, less than half a man's height, and Durell swung it open and gestured them inside. The dark cubbyhole within was rancid with sweat and blood.

"In there," Durell ordered.

They crowded backward into the tiny cubbyhole. Their eyes gleamed like vicious animals as Durell slammed the small door shut on them and threw the bolt. He turned his gun back on Tai Ma. The fat man had not moved.

"You are foolish, Shan—if that is your name. What do you propose to do with me? It is a matter of logistics, of my physical size. You cannot crowd me in with my assistants."

Durell ignored him and went to the table. Chien Y-Wu's eyes were closed. His breathing was too fast, and the thud of his laboring heart was visible through his ribs. Bubbles of saliva oozed from his ashen lips.

"General Chien?"

"He has fainted," Tai Ma said blandly.

But the victim's slanted eyelids fluttered, the shocked eyes looked up at the naked light bulb. Durell tapped the cord and made the light swing back and forth above the man's face. He made his voice gentle and suddenly spoke in English.

"I am a friend, but I can't help you unless you decide to cooperate, Chien."

"W-what? I don't—understand——"

"Just answer my questions."

"Are you going to kill me?"

"It depends."

"I wish—I wish to live——" The man began to weep.

"Tell me about the Six Sentinels," Durell said.

Tai Ma made a sighing sound. "You are not Shan, are you? I have been studying your face. I have considered Shan's dossiers. It is very, very good. Very clever. But you are not Shan."

"Stand over there, Tai."

The fat man moved silently to the wall, his ponderous body poised. Durell kept his gun ready. He heard a gong and the whisper of the air-conditioner. There was a smell of vomit and blood from Chien Y-Wu on the surgical table.

"Who told you defect, Chien?" he asked quietly.

"I had orders. They came through Colonel Chu."

"Chu? And who did he work for?"

"The—the little man. K Section."

"Name him," Durell said.

"Dickinson McFee. General Dickinson McFee."

"McFee ordered you to defect?"

"Yes."

"And ordered you to give L-5 our electronic secrets?"

"Yes."

"Why?"

"I do not know."

"You do know. Hurry. Answer me."

"There is talk—whispers—of a secret cabal, some men who call themselves the Six Sentinels—Americans, high officers in the military and government——"

"Name them," Durell snapped.

"I do not know them! I swear! You can kill me——"

"You named McFee."

"Chu gave me his name."

"No others?"

"I do not know the others."

The air-conditioner went off. A voice chattered softly on the intercom on Tai Ma's desk. Durell did not catch the words. Nothing changed in Tai Ma's face. Chien's breathing grew worse, and Durell leaned over the man's spasmed face. "Answer these questions. Can you hear me, Chien?"

"I—hear you."

"Who is White Guard?"

"The President—of the United States."

"And Dragon?"

There was silence.

"Dragon?" Durell repeated.

"General—General Dickinson McFee."

"You lie!"

The tormented face was the color of old suet. "No. Please. Get me a doctor. I am in terrible pain."

"Who is Dragon?"

"McFee."

"He sent you to Peking?"

"Yes."

"Why? Tell me again."

"To give—electronic data—on espionage equipment."

"Why?" Durell repeated.

"To give—this regime—in Peking, an excuse——"

The victim coughed and strangled. The body jerked and twitched on the table. Overhead, the lamp flickered, grew dim, then brightened again.

Chien whispered, "To provoke the regime—into a retaliation—which would give an excuse for an atomic—return. Nuclear war—would result. Taiwan would be—the alibi. The Six Sentinels feel—a war now—preventive—would be best. Later, Red China will be—too strong—for the United States——"

"Name the Six Sentinels," Durell insisted.

"I—cannot."

"Do you wish to die now?"

"I know only two others——"

"Who are they?"

Chien opened his mouth, coughed, and started to speak. There was a blur of movement in the corner of Durell's eye. Tai Ma came away from the wall of the cell, where he had been watching and listening, with all the impetus of a wild buffalo's charge. The momentum of his enormous weight barreled into Durell and the table like an avalanche. Durell was hurled across the room, caromed off the desk, and came up in a crouch. Tai Ma's huge face was expressionless. Something glittered, flickered in his stubby fingers, vanished into the prisoner's heaving, scrawny chest. It was a sleeve knife. Durell had no chance to stop the murder. There was a gout of blood, a whispering sigh as Chien collapsed like a thin sack of air, and then the table went over between Durell and the huge L-5 man.

"If you shoot me," Tai Ma breathed quickly, "all the alarms will go off."

Durell's finger was tight on the trigger. His right arm trembled slightly; he had slammed it against the desk when Tai Ma hurled him aside.

"Be reasonable," Tai Ma whispered. "You and I can reach an understanding."

"Did you kill him?"

"I hope so."

"He was about to tell you what you wanted to know."

"I already know what the dog would say."

"And you didn't want me to hear it?"

"You are not Shan. I do not know who you are. So you must die—quickly."

The man's knife flickered like the tongue of a snake. Durell stepped between the fat man and the cell door. He heard no alarm from the tunnel outside, but he knew that somehow Tai Ma had alerted the guards. Perhaps he had used a buzzer under his desk, or opened a listening device in the torture cell. There was a hissing sound from the air-conditioner then, and a white vapor curled around the electric bulb strung from the ceiling.

Durell's toe prodded Chien's body, which had been hurled from the table by Tai's violent attack. Chien was dead. Tai's knife had pierced the heart with expert efficiency, and he saw bright arterial blood on the knife blade that now stabbed and thrust at him. No time now to wonder if Chien's death could have been prevented. He heard a hammering from the small cell door where he had imprisoned the Manchurians. They had sensed a change in the situation. Durell backed toward the main door, and Tai came around the overturned table, grinning suddenly, tasting triumph in Durell's retreat.

"You understand?" the Chinese said softly. "You have lost. You were lost from the beginning, from before you even took Shan's place."

"Why do you think I'm not Shan?"

"There are differences. You do not fit Shan's pattern."

Durell nodded. "You will take me out of here."

"True. To the morgue, with the running dog of an imperialist I just killed. You must drop your gun. It is stupid of you to resist."

The air vent hissed again. The vapor was getting thicker, but it was lighter than air and did not settle quickly. There was a trace of ammonia in the air, however, and Durell breathed lightly and shallowly. Tai Ma laughed.

"The gas is not deadly. It will only make us pass out. After that, you will take Chien's place. The Manchurians will be happy to exercise their ancient talents on your body."

"I can always kill you first," Durell said flatly. He raised his gun and saw surprise on Tai's round face. Durell squeezed the trigger. The shot was deafening in the narrow confines of the cell. The fat man went down like an oak chopped off at the base of the trunk. Durell had aimed correctly at the right knee. Tai's face spasmed and then froze with pain. His hands went flat on the stone wall and slid down, his leg twisted under him; he bit his lip until blood came, and his slanted eyes looked at Durell incredulously. Then he fainted.

Durell took a careful step toward him, his gun aimed at Tai's head every moment while he pulled back the fat man's eyelids and checked. Tai Ma was out cold. He straightened slowly, and when he was a safe three steps away, he thrust his gun in his belt and turned swiftly to the iron cell door.

It was locked. There was no keyhole and no key. It operated electronically. He turned back to the desk, ducked under the kneehole, and found the button and pressed it. Nothing happened, and he was filled with dread lest he be trapped here.

Then, with a low whine, the door slid aside.

He stepped out quickly. From around a bend in the tunnel came high, querulous voices, raised in alarm. No one was in sight yet. He turned away from the sounds and trotted quickly down the visible length of the tunnel before him. There were several cell doors, all open. He turned a corner and the tunnel became less modern, walled with old brick. Darkness loomed beyond the last string of lights. He sprinted for it, heard a shout behind him. The old part of the tunnel, which could lead him anywhere under Peking toward the Imperial City, was about a hundred yards ahead, under the vaulted ceiling. He ran through a long pool of water, splashing noisily. A high-pitched buzzing alarm went off, piercing the tunnel with echoes. A loudspeaker gave out a spate of orders. Suddenly, from a side tunnel, several guards spilled into view. Their automatic weapons were at hip-level, and they began to fire as soon as they saw him.

He threw himself flat, saw a door a few yards ahead, and crawled rapidly for it. Brick chips and dust sprayed in his eyes, scratched his face. The roar of automatic fire was deafening. He reached the door and rolled inside, not caring where he landed as long as he was out of tunnel, which was like a shooting gallery with himself as a running target.

He was in the anteroom of what looked like an elevator shaft. The elevator door, with its unmistakable row of buttons, was closed. He lunged up, desperate, and punched the first button, then flattened against the wall, breathing lightly and quickly, his head turned to watch the door to the tunnel.

The elevator whined, but there were no indicators to tell him how far above him the cage might be. Hope faded as the firing in the tunnel ended. He heard the cautious scuffle of approaching feet near the door. He could never get out in time. The gun butt felt slippery with sweat in his hands. There were only moments left——

The elevator door slid softly aside.

He heard a whisper of command from the men just beyond the anteroom and side-stepped, still watching the door as he eased into the brightly modern cage. He could not possibly see if anyone was in the elevator; his attention was fixed on the gun muzzle being cautiously poked around the corner.

He was aware of a flat sound behind his ear, of a blur of movement in the corner of his eye, of a face beside the elevator door. Light exploded behind his eyes. Pain smashed him down to his knees. His gun went off reflexively, firing shot after shot into the elevator floor. He tried to raise it, to focus on the image that towered above him. The face was familiar. He saw it smiling down at him from a vast height.

It was Colonel Chu, the Lotus pilot of the KMT who had flown him into China.

His last thought was that Chu had been forced to crash, after he and Jasmine had jumped by parachute.

Then he saw the gun in Chu's hand, descending slowly as if impeded by the drag of deep water. The whirling, dizzying light burst in his brain once more, and then he pitched forward out of the elevator, down an endless, black shaft that dropped him into nowhere.

Thirteen

HE SWEATED, BUT HE FELT COLD. HIS EYES WERE open, but he saw nothing. He lay on something hard, and metal thrust into his ribs, and yet he floated gently in a nothing world of no-thought and no-feeling. Then his head ached, but his thoughts seemed crystal-clear.

He looked up into Colonel Chu's young, benign face.

"I never thought," said Chu, "you would get this far."

"Why not?"

"It was arranged to stop you."

"And you finally had to do it yourself?"

Chu smiled. "You shattered Tai Ma's kneecap. For a man of his size, it will be a lifelong disability."

"I should have killed him."

"As you killed Chien Y-Wu?"

"Tai Ma did that."

"So?"

"Precisely. So."

Chu hit him in the face. The pain of the blow seemed to sort out his detached thoughts and put them in order again. His senses began to work normally again. The hard cot under him was filled with springs; the darkness went. He saw Chu's narrow yellow face shadowed by a brightly glaring light behind him. What he could make out of the room looked like a duplicate of the torture cell where Chien had died; but he couldn't be sure of this, and he didn't concern himself about it. When he tried to sit up, he found he was fastened to the cot by leather straps at both wrists and both ankles and a wide leather band across his chest. He felt blood in his mouth.

Colonel Chu smiled pleasantly and rubbed his knuckles. "You are not surprised to see me here in the Black House?"

"Nothing surprises me now."

"You were betrayed from the start, you see. Your mission was aborted before it was properly originated."

"I knew that."

"This is why you were reluctant to go, back on Taiwan?"

"I never trusted you," Durell said. "How long have you been working for Peking?"

"Always. Since I left the Chinese mainland." Chu lit a cigarette with delicate gestures. He wore racing driver's gloves, the fingers exposed, long and tapering. "You really should not have killed Chien, you know. We wanted more information from him."

"Tai Ma did it with his little switchblade."

"Do not provoke me with lies. You have no hope for mercy unless you cooperate with me." Chu walked back and forth in the narrow cell. The light reflected glossily from his slick black hair, his youthful face, his thin moustache and somewhat pouting mouth. He had been speaking in English, Durell suddenly realized, and now he saw in a corner of the room an elaborate tape recorder that had been dutifully taking down Durell's replies. But Chu was different from the rather foppish, effeminate KMT flight officer Durell had known in Taiwan. There was a sense of power and assurance that had not been there before. Durell was grateful for the ebbing of the pain in his head from Chu's blow. He turned his head and the movement pulled at the blood caked on the back of his neck. He tested the leather straps tentatively. He couldn't move in any direction on the table.

"How can I cooperate?" he asked quietly.

Chu turned sharply, and his black eyes gazed down at him with utter lack of passion. "You have been given into my hands. No one in the Black House understands your significance as a catalyst except myself. Do you know what that means?"

"I'm going to die," Durell said simply.

"Yes. The question that remains is simply how it will happen. Easily and quickly—or slowly and hard? No one here knows your true identity—not even Tai Ma, who is clever and dangerous, but not completely informed." Chu's brief smile meant nothing. "Tai does not know I am one of the Six Sentinels he seeks. Chien did not know it, either. I do not believe that even your former chief, General McFee, who betrayed you, knows it—although I do not discount that man's capacities."

"If you're a Sentinel, whose side are you on?"

"These are difficult times. It is easy for a man to lose his head. One cannot trade safety for ideals in this modern world, or be a martyr to any cause. One must be pragmatic. Today's deathless 'cause' becomes only an uninteresting item in tomorrow's history, and the man who dies for such a cause is a fool. I plan to live a long and comfortable life."

"You won't," Durell said.

"Do you still threaten me, helpless as you are?"

"It's a statement of fact."

"You sound stupidly certain of yourself."

Durell tested his ankle straps. It was hopeless. "What do you want of me, Chu?"

"I have reconsidered your role in this affair. You have actually accomplished part of your mission. Chien is dead and silenced. Therefore, you must be my source of information. However carefully I tried, I never was able to capture and inspect one of the Zebra Program mechanisms."

"The what?"

Chu's eyes were bleak. "Chien Y-Wu did not know what or how they were made, or by what electronics company in the States. We tested his reactions carefully to all this. His information and the schematic drawings he yielded were all of routine electronic espionage mechanisms. Nowhere was there a hint of the Zebra device. We thought he might have some data on it, but nothing he said gave us a hint about it."

"The 'Zebra device?' "

"Do you pretend to be ignorant about it?"

"I never heard it mentioned. You attended my briefings."

Chu's mouth tightened. "Do not toy with me, I warn you. You will die hard, and beg me for death when it comes!" He drew a quick breath. "I give you thirty minutes only. You could know much, or nothing. I believe you were secretly briefed in Washington on your true assignment here. Your value—and the time remaining of your life, and whether you go easily or in utmost agony —depends on you."

Durell saw a thin sheen of sweat on Chu's youthful face. His petulant mouth showed a dangerous lack of patience.

"All right, I'll cooperate," Durell said. He watched Chu's mouth twitch slightly. "But tell me what *you* know of the Zebra program. As far as all the others are concerned, it's merely a flight program over mainland China for aerial high-altitude photography and intelligence-gathering missions."

Chu regarded him for a silent moment. "I think you are pulling a crude bluff. And yet you are a subtle and dangerous man, Durell. A bluff within a bluff? I cannot tell." He smiled. "I confess my uneasiness readily, as you see."

"You can afford to," Durell said.

Chu paced up and down the cell. He spoke quickly and tersely, sticking to his Oxonian English. The Zebra program over the mainland was a cover for dropping and establishing the Zebra device to trusted agents of the KMT and the National Security Agency under General Haystead's command. So far, none of the devices had been recovered by the Black House counterespionage apparatus in Peking. Great advances had been made in the miniaturization of listening devices tuned to an infinitely small and remarkably powerful transmitter planted at the site of the objective. It was known that some of the Chinese government's innermost secret conferences had been recorded by Zebra, from many miles away.

"You've been taken," Durell said, interrupting.

"How so?"

"No such gadget has been developed yet. It's still in the laboratory stage in the basement at K Section's headquarters."

"But it is in Haystead's hands——"

"It is in McFee's hands, not the NSA's."

Chu looked confused. "But my information——"

"You've been misled. Our business is like the shell game run by a carnival trickster. Now you see it, now you don't. It was decided that although the Zebra Program was designed for ultimate use of the device, no one was to know of it until it was ready. And it is not ready. It has not been used."

"You lie to me!" Chu shouted. He took a quick step toward the table, and his long, strong fingers began manipulating the cords of Durell's throat. Pain exploded in his skull like bursting skyrockets. A groan escaped his clenched teeth. He bit his tongue and tasted blood. It was only the beginning, he knew, of Chu's immoderate temper. And it had to be provoked further. He had to induce Chu to knock him out, and quickly. He spoke through the blood in his mouth.

"You've been suckered, Chu, just like me, just like most of us in the business. The people on top use us, betray us, sacrifice us—for their own ends—most of which are wildly improbable adventures that cost only our own lives, not theirs, and bolster their own egos and positions. You think you are one of the Six Sentinels? How do you know? Maybe it was just a gimmick to make you perform better for the real brains behind this plot to provoke Red China into a nuclear attack on Taiwan—and in turn, cause American nuclear retaliation. Peking thinks it's big enough to survive such a holocaust—but not with the hell bombs and germ warfare and every other demoniacal mechanism that certain madmen, in the fury of war, will try out. You don't know which end is up, Chu. Chien Y-Wu was never important. The Zebra Program is only a cover. You and I are only being used as cat's-paws, to torture and kill each other for purposes we can only guess at."

Chu took a tremulous breath and looked at his airman's wristwatch. Durell licked blood from his lips as the man said, "I am only interested in personal survival. I despise you, Durell. Your patriotism is well known, although you conceal it always behind a cynical façade. You shall not provoke me. You will tell me more of the Zebra device."

"Are you afraid?" Durell asked quietly.

"Afraid? Of what?"

"You've been with the KMT too long, and no one trusts you here. Anyone who's been abroad and in the upper echelons of capitalist society is suspect here in Peking. They can't really trust you. You must deliver something to them, right? Something to prove your value to the Black House. You hope to get it from me. But you won't. You're going to die along with me, Chu. If you kill me, you're finished, too. Make up your mind to it."

Chu turned pale under his yellow skin, and his dark eyes glittered. His fist smashed Durell on the jaw, and as Durell's head snapped aside, he felt his face ground into the hard table to which he was strapped. His body spasmed, his muscles strained, and the strap on his left wrist suddenly gave way. His fist swung in a wild arc and slammed into Chu's throat, his knuckles extended like a handful of pebbles striking flesh. Chu twisted and staggered away, clutching his neck with both hands, coughing and retching. Durell desperately reached with his left hand to undo his right. Chu, bent double, slowly turned back to the table. Their eyes met, and Chu's hooded glare was insane with frustrated rage. His glance slid to the humming tape recorder, and horror touched his eyes. He brought his fist down three times on the machine, smashing it into immobility. Then he came forward to the table again.

"Very well," he gasped hoarsely. "You made your decision. You will die with me."

He locked his fists together and brought them down, like a maul, on Durell's face. Durell's last thought was one of satisfaction. If he lived through this, he at least could not be made to talk. Then the blow struck, and again he knew nothing more.

Fourteen

HE AWOKE TO A FEEBLE LIGHT GLOWING FAR OFF IN the distance. A woman's voice said in Cantonese, "Major Shan, please wake up. It is all right. You are safe. Wake up."

The thin light blinded him and stabbed pain into his head. He breathed with difficulty—blood clotted his nasal passages. He felt a warm, wet cloth applied to his face, which felt swollen, like his tongue in his bloody mouth.

"Shan, darling?"

The voice was familiar; the urgency was not unexpected. He had an instant of *deja vu*, as if he had been here before. He tried to move and found he had been freed of the straps that had bound him to the table when Chu was questioning him. How much time had passed since then? He could not guess. His mind felt numbed, still shocked by the massive blow Chu had delivered.

"Shan, please!"

Now fear mingled with the urgency of the woman's voice. He opened his eyes again. The feeble light became a glow that took the shape of a curved, brick doorway, a wet stone slab floor. He heard other sounds now. Running feet. A distant shout. He was in an alcove of one of the old Imperial tunnels, lying in two inches of slowly trickling water that smelled like a fetid sewer. He shuddered and immediately felt a strong young arm lift him up.

"Can you hear me at all, Shan?"

"I hear you," he whispered.

"Oh, good! Can you stand up?"

"Doubt it," he mumbled.

"You must! There is no time left."

All at once he knew the voice. "Jasmine?"

"Yes, I'm here, darling. Darling, look at me. Oh, your

poor face! They'll be coming here soon. I can't drag you any farther, I just can't."

"Colonel Chu——"

"I hit him. I think he's dead, but I'm not sure."

"Shouldn't have. He knows—things. He——"

"Get up. Please! Now!"

He summoned all his strength and lifted himself to his knees. His head rang with a million bells. His stomach lurched, and he threw up like a child. The nausea passed. Jasmine tugged at him. "On your feet, *please!*"

He heard the sounds of searching men nearby. "How did you find me?"

He saw her face now, in the dim light. She wore some kind of black cotton women's uniform. Her long, black hair was pulled back into a severe bun. Her eyes were luminous with the pressure of fear, but she smiled and said, "Didn't Chu ask you about a Zebra listening device?"

"How did you know that?"

"Because it exists. I heard everything. We planted one of the mechanisms in his ball-point pen. He never knew it, never suspected. He wanted to have one desperately, to deliver to his masters here, but the joke was on him. The move was dangerous, but I had to know where Chu was, at all times."

He said grimly, "You know a lot more than I, Jasmine. Did you take the pen back?"

"Yes."

"Give it to me."

She hesitated, briefly enough to kindle every wild suspicion he'd ever entertained about her, and then she handed him an innocuous-looking pen, the sort that are made by the millions. He put it away in an inside pocket of his battered cotton suit. His gun was gone, he noted. So was his watch and every other personal item that identified him as Major Shan, of L-5's Black House. He wouldn't get far, he decided grimly. But he had to try.

He got to his feet. The tunnel expanded and swayed and rotated in his dizziness. He clung to Jasmine.

"How can we get out?"

"The same way I came in. Hao had only a partial map of these tunnels. There's one unused section that connects with the Black House complex. This way. To the left. Hurry!"

He managed to put one foot ahead of the other and stumble along with Jasmine's help. Lights flickered behind them some distance away. He could not have been unconscious very long—half an hour at the most, he guessed. With each step, he regained a small measure of his strength, although his knees felt like rubber and his face throbbed. He did not know if Chu had broken his nose or not. He seemed to swim uphill against a dark river of pain, following Jasmine's tall figure in her dark, utilitarian uniform, feeling the strong, cool pressure of her hand as she led him. She had saved him once before, in Singapore, he remembered, when he had gone after the notorious Madame Hung. Now, risking her life again, she was leading him to safety once more. And still he did not trust her. His long term of service in K Section had made him somewhat less than human, he reflected dully. He had given up a normal capacity for trust and friendship and replaced it with a minute-to-minute awareness of death and danger. You trusted no one, you depended on no one.

He checked his stumbling progress.

"Where are we going?"

"It's a long way yet." Jasmine breathed with difficulty.

"Where can we be safe? I've something I must do——"

"Hao will help us. He's a little wonder. He's one of McFee's most trusted people here——"

"He takes orders from McFee? But I thought——"

He fell silent, reflecting that she could not put him into any greater danger than that from which he had just escaped. He stumbled on, up a ramplike section of the old brick tunnel that grew narrower and darker with each step. They had taken several careful turns where the tunnels forked, when Jasmine halted and searched her memory for the way. Now the shafts were totally dark, and they had been proceeding for some time by following the walls with their hands. The smell of sewage, rat droppings, and other indefinable odors, had grown thicker. They waded through ankle-deep water, over the stone floor that was slippery with slime. The air tasted heavy and dead.

The way seemed endless. The tunnels formed a maze without beginning or end. For a time, he feared Jasmine was leading him in dark circles—but she did not falter long, except to take her time at intersections to make certain of their course.

Now and then he had to pause for rest. His face ached more savagely with each passing minute, and he wondered if any damage had been done to the plastic silicone-filled sacs that Dr. Greentree had inserted to round out his features to the accepted Chinese conformation.

"We're almost there," Jasmine said thinly.

"We've lost the Black House men," he said encouragingly.

"Yes, but these tunnels go on for miles——"

"You're doing fine."

"Are you all right?" she asked.

"Better every minute. Here's a stairway, I think."

She halted, came back, bumped into him in the darkness. Her hair still had the essence of her identifying perfume, brushing against him as she squeezed into a dark crevice in the crumbling brick wall. Water trickled under their fingers as they felt their way along the invisible, rubbled stairway.

She breathed with relief. "Yes, this is it."

"Where does it take us?"

"Up into about a million people," she said.

Now and then the steps vanished in a slide of debris that was treacherous underfoot. There was absolutely nothing to see for several moments as they labored upward. Once Jasmine slipped and started to slide down with a small cry. He caught her wrist in the dark and held her tight. She lay there for some minutes, breathing quickly and unevenly.

"Thanks, Sam."

"I owe you my life again," he said.

"We're not home safe yet."

The stairs angled to the left. Durell's hands were bleeding as he scrabbled upward on the broken brick. He guessed they had gone several miles from the area of the Black House, and his sense of direction, even in the blackness, suggested that they might be under the palaces of the Forbidden City.

Suddenly there was a gray glimmering ahead and above. At the same time, he became aware of sound, like the rise and fall of a far-off sea. It took a moment for him to realize that he was hearing, even at this subterranean level, the measured shouts and tramping of half a million people gathered at the great Gate of Heavenly Peace at the entrance to the Imperial Palaces. It was National Day in full progress.

As they climbed, the light became a thin slit of gray gloom, a vertical line about the height of a door panel. Distance was deceptive. They came upon it moments before he expected it.

Jasmine paused. "We must be absolutely still. We're under the Hall of Earthly Tranquillity." Her face was dusty and ashen from their long tour through the ancient tunnels. "There are dozens of courtyards here that Hao showed me, not far from the Chunghotien, the Hall of Complete Harmony. It was once used by the emperors as a resting place on their way to the Throne Room. There's a golden roof, and triple terraces, and a great central building, all surrounded by smaller palaces, and halls and courtyards once occupied as residences for members of the Imperial family and their concubines."

"You've had quite a tour," Durell said.

"I was briefed for it," she said shortly. "Well, we can't stay here. Keep your fingers crossed that some delegation from Pakistan or Africa isn't standing around."

She pushed lightly on the panel that she had left ajar. It moved outward easily, for some ten inches, then stuck. She made a small sound, then said, "We'll squeeze through."

"I'll go first," he offered.

When he stepped through, the light almost blinded him. Jasmine pressed quickly after him. He saw that what he had taken to be her uniform was really a dark blue cotton suit, with a brightly designed scarf and an embroidered blouse. Somehow, despite her dishevelment, she looked lovely and smart.

Now he heard the swelling roar and marching of feet like some great tidal wave, martial in sound, disciplined in its distantly shouted slogans from thousands of simultaneous throats. He found himself in a small room paneled in bright vermilion, with yellow-timbered ceilings and openings that yielded onto a paved court with twisted, stunted trees, enormous flower beds, and elaborately carved marble bridges. An artificial waterfall tinkled dimly through the distant uproar.

"Oh, Sam—your face! If you're seen——"

He grinned. "Not good enough to be shown to the past and present glories of the Middle Kingdom and the People's Republic?"

"Don't joke. We'll never make it. The streets are jammed, and we have to get to the Summer Palace to meet Hao, and by now, Tai Ma will be scouring the city for us."

"Come along," he said.

He stepped out of the vermilion room into the intimate little court with its marble bridge and fountain. It felt empty, as if the ordinary tourists who swarmed through this vast splendor of history had been barred during today's celebrations. He was surprised to find it was still early in the afternoon. He had been in the Black House since dawn, some six hours, and rain still fell from gray skies; it was made colder by an icy wind that rippled the artificial pond and sent a fine spray from the waterfall. He knelt by the pool and considered his reflection in the water. The battered face of Shan stared back at him, bloody, dusty, and swollen. His blue cotton suit was not too bad—the tears in the sleeve and shoulder could be hidden enough to avoid comment. But his face . . .

"Let me help," said Jasmine.

She took her colored scarf and dipped it into the pool and then bathed Durell's eyes and nose. The cold water smarted. There were tears in the girl's eyes as she knelt and tended to his wounds. "Oh, I'm sorry I couldn't help you sooner! But when you didn't come back, I made Hao tell me how to reach you."

"Why didn't Hao tell me how to get in that way before?"

"I don't think he knew. I think he just discovered it, himself, after you left."

He said abruptly, "Jasmine, what am I being set up for?"

"I don't understand."

"I'm being used—shaped, molded, brainwashed. You name it. I'm being led into something, I'm not sure what—"

"I don't know, Sam," she said.

"No other job was like this. Why did McFee assign you to watch me? What's he afraid I might do?"

She made no reply. His face felt better for the cold water, and he could breathe again through his nose; he decided that Chu had not broken it after all. His face still looked like a reasonable facsimile of Major Shan's. He drank some of the fountain water, suddenly accepting thirst and hunger as signs that he was better. The thin rain had soaked through his clothes, and he saw that Jasmine was shivering.

"Let's go."

She gave him an appraising look. "I guess you'll do. If this were anywhere else in the world, you could pretend to be drunk. But not in Peking today. The first passerby would take it as his citizen's duty to upbraid you for nonsocialist, demoralizing, weak behavior."

They walked briskly, as if on urgent business. There were sheafs of flags stuck in sconces in the hallway they traversed, and Durell took two of the banners and gave one to Jasmine. One was red, the other yellow and blue, and they were inscribed with the mottos, UNITE AND CARE FOR EACH OTHER and SOCIALISM IS GOOD. The flapping banners helped conceal the bedraggled state of their clothing.

A hubbub of voices sounded ahead. They came into a great audience hall, a dream of timber colored deep saffron and red, lofty and airy. Long outdoor walks led to wide terraces facing the Palace Grounds. The hall was filled with uniformed schoolgirls with placards, waiting their place in the march. In the light rain, Durell glimpsed incredible masses of people marching through the Gate of Heavenly Peace, which stood like an enormous fortress, eighty feet thick, with carmine walls. Atop the gate were the dignitaries of the Chinese People's Republic, watching the massed thousands parade through the hundred-acre concourse. He thought wryly that the Ming Emperors, who had thrown out the Mongol dynasty established by Genghis Khan, could not have conceived of this spectacle before their autocratic, divine eyes. From the top of the terrace, as he pushed through the waiting marchers with Jasmine's hand in his, he saw a vista of multiple roofs in turquoise and sapphire, upright lines of tall wooden pillars beneath amber arabesques upturned to the rain. Shrubs flowered everywhere, and for the occasion, along every marble pavilion, there were huge tubs of chrysanthemums, cannas, and cyclamen to add to the color of the festival.

The sound was enormous. The powerful politicians atop the Gate looked minute, waving tiny arms in automatic gestures to the troops of marchers going by in the huge square.

"This way," Jasmine called above the noise.

They pushed through ranks of workers who gave them annoyed looks. Jasmine tightened her grip on his hand, as if afraid she might lose him in this frightening, organized sea of humanity. Turning left, she squeezed through a small gate in terra-cotta walls and paused under the dark branches of dripping cypress trees. An elaborate, circular pavilion with Chinese gingerbread doors and roofs stood before them.

"Through here."

Looking back, Durell saw a massive Red Star of China being carried by a new segment of marchers. Their chanted slogans shook the air and sounded obscene among the delicate elegances of this fantasy of palace, pavilion, terrace, and walls.

"Hurry, Shan!"

They raced along covered walkways, with mossy marble floors, doubled back along empty pathways, gardens, and marble bridges, and suddenly debouched on a small side street. Durell realized that she had led him accurately and speedily out of the Forbidden City and the massed festival marchers. The rain beat down coldly. They abandoned their camouflage of sloganed flags and started around a corner, saw a trolley bursting with uniformed children, waited while a battalion of blue-uniformed militia marched by, ignored a vender's plea to buy paper flowers, and waited under a huge, round scarlet lantern.

Jasmine looked exhausted. "He's not here."

"Are you waiting for Hao?"

"One of his aides. He—no, there he is."

Durell watched for any sign of Tai Ma's people, who were surely turning the city upside down in a desperate search for him; but in these crowded, exuberant streets, it was impossible to pick out anyone who might be an L-5 agent. He watched a float go by, then another, wheeling slowly around the corner in the direction from which they had come. Martial music sounded briefly through the rain. Banners hung limp, dripping, then flapped and sent a sharp, icy spattering down upon them.

"Here. Oh, good," Jasmine murmured.

A rare motorcar on Peking's streets eased between the floats and headed for them as they stood under a dripping tree on the sidewalk. It was a Polish Warszawa, dull black, driven by a thin, scholarly-looking Chinese.

"It's Jen Feng-Bao. He teaches Japanese at Peking University. He works with Hao."

They got in and the driver nodded, smiled, and then set his mouth in tense anxiety as he eased the Warszawa away from the curb. In a moment, they were on an emptier boulevard, lined with young trees, fighting the tides of people sucked as if by a siphon toward the reviewing stands at the Gate of Heavenly Peace.

"You are fortunate," the driver said. "One did not really expect you to be successful, Jasmine."

"Has there been any trouble?"

"I monitored L-5's radio. Of course there is trouble. The most insignificant ant, if he tunnels just right, can topple a mountain," Jen Feng-Bao smiled.

They headed for the Summer Palace, under festive trees that defied the cold rain with enormous, fringed scarlet lanterns and more posters and banners hailing the Party leaders. Jen drove carefully, with academic precision. In twenty minutes they entered the 800-acre grounds of the Summer Palace. There were over one hundred buildings here, and on normal days the halls and temples would be swarming with sightseers at their ease. Built by the Ming Emperor, K'ang Hsi, in the seventeenth century, and enlarged with more modern buildings by Ch'ien Lung, the area had been restored to its former splendor that not even the dismal rain could hide. The small Warszawa swung along empty drives toward the Buddhist "Sea of Wisdom" temple on its artificial hill overlooking a wide, man-made lake. Scarlet and emerald timbers flickered by; the painted boats for public use lay in tidy, idle rows this day. The wind was stronger, the rain colder, the trees and shrubbery bowed before the desolation of the day.

Jasmine leaned forward. "Do you see him, Jen?"

"Not yet."

They passed tinkling waterfalls, lakes full of blossoms, and the Dowager Empress's marble barge in its shallow pond. They halted briefly near the Hall of Listening to the Birds, again at the Hall of Virtuous Harmony.

"There," Jen said with sudden relief.

Hurrying toward them, under a preposterously large black umbrella, was the slight, gray-robed figure of the monk. Hao got in quickly, looked at Durell's face. "There has been much trouble. They—ah—questioned you?"

"Somewhat. Is your temple still safe?"

"Yes, we go there at once." The monk was agitated. His eyes did not meet Durell's. "Nothing happens as we plan, under the Eye of Heaven. Heaven cares nothing for mortal man and our hopes. We have problems."

"That's an understatement," Durell said dryly.

Hao leaned forward to speak over the driver's shoulder. His hands trembled. Until now, since Wuhan, he had been calm. Now he said to the driver, "Be very careful. Circle three times. Make sure we are not seen. Otherwise, we must go to the country, do you understand? And I cannot have you under suspicion, Jen. It would destroy everything. My own life has little value, but you would have to take command after me."

"I understand," Jen said.

Durell said quietly: "What's happened?"

Hao's eyes searched Durell's battered face. "Do you need medical attention? You look different to me."

"A few bruises only. How do you mean, different?"

"Forgive me, I've had a shock. You will understand when we arrive."

The little temple and its hidden court, set among the streets of old Peking that the regime had not yet cleared for more workers' barracks, looked secure and familiar as the Warszawa swung around the corner. Hao, Jasmine, and Durell got out in the rain and watched as the professor waved and drove off.

"Inside," Hao said.

They crossed the courtyard to the little apartment behind the temple. An old sweeping woman in a traditional, high-collared tunic, with trousers and black cotton shoes, bowed and handed Hao a copy of the *Renmin Ribao*—the *People's Daily*. The little monk folded it and handed it back. He looked pale. Hao said something too quickly for Durell to catch, and the woman's almond eyes slewed to Durell. This time he did not miss the expression in her eyes. They reflected shock and disbelief.

"What's the trouble, Hao?"

"Nothing. All is well."

"What's the old woman afraid of?"

"She was surprised to see you, that is all."

Hao led the way into the apartment that had served them for the past ten days. It seemed to Durell he had been away for a long time since going to the Black House. Nothing was changed in the sitting-room or kitchen. There was a new rush mat on the stone floor, a table with four wooden chairs under a window that looked out on the temple court, an alarm clock, and one of the Chinese Thermos bottles in bright green with an ugly floral design painted on it. On the single-ring gas stove was a stew of pork and fish and vegetables, sliced with the razor-sharp chopper dear to all Chinese housewives. A fistful of North China's favorite steamed bread stood on the wooden table, as if someone had been eating there and had just put it down.

Durell picked up the kitchen chopper at the stove. The room seemed dark, surrounded by the walled court outside, veiled by the lowering clouds that swept over Peking.

"All right, Hao. Level with me."

Hao wrung his hands. "I do not know what to do."

Jasmine stood with Durell. "Something's wrong. Someone else is here, isn't that right, Hao?"

"Yes. Yes, indeed."

"Who is it?" Durell asked. "Why do you all look at me as if I were a ghost?"

"You shall see for yourself. In there."

Hao gestured to the tiny bedroom that Durell had shared earlier with Jasmine. The painted yellow door was closed. Suddenly he wished he had a weapon better than the chopper. His stomach curled with apprehension, and then he yanked open the door.

There was a single oil lamp inside, reflecting on the polished stone floor. A man sat on the edge of the bed, his back to Durell. He had heavy shoulders, thick black hair, an air of tension in the way he held his body, a smooth coordination of nerve and muscle under his simple cotton suit. He stood up, the bedsprings creaking, still with his back to Durell.

"Hello, Major Shan," the man said.

Then he turned, and Durell looked at an identical reflection of his own image.

Fifteen

THERE WAS A MOMENT OF MUTUAL SHOCK AS THEY stared at each other. The apartment was utterly silent. Then Durell heard the gurgling of rain in the ceramic eaves, the splash of the courtyard fountain, a sudden hissing of steam as the old woman put on a tea kettle in the kitchen. Durell watched the other man—himself—smile tightly. He smiled in return. Neither moved, studying each other with awe. Durell's estimate of the job that Ike Greentree had done on his face soared to gratification. At the same time, he was staring at a man supposed to be long dead.

"Major Shan?" he asked finally.

"Precisely. And you, too, are Major Shan. That makes two of us." The other's voice was a little higher in pitch than his own. "You are surprised? So am I. Hao told me about you, but I could not believe it. It is remarkable, eh? We are twins. Identical in all appearances."

"Skin deep, only," Durell said. He spoke harshly. "Where did you come from?"

"Obviously not from the grave." The Chinese smiled ruefully, his black eyes continuing to regard Durell with awe. "I was prepared for this; you were not. But I admire your control, Sam Durell. They call you the Cajun, do they not? I have read your L-5 dossiers, of course. Your abilities were not exaggerated."

"Have you a weapon?" Durell asked.

"I am not armed. You may search me."

Durell did so, still holding the kitchen chopper. The man's body was thinner than his, even wasted; he was trembling slightly, but Durell did not think it was from fear. Durell was about an inch taller; the real Shan's face was somewhat broader, his eyes longer; there was a series of small scars on his left cheek. Perhaps that was what Tai Ma had suddenly noticed in the Black House. It was the only difference in features between them, except for Durell's current lumps and bruises.

Shan's clothing was empty of weapons.

"All right," Durell said. "Sit down again. You have a lot to explain."

"So have you, Cajun."

"We were assured you were dead."

"And I am not." The man's voice was calm. He sat on the wooden chair in the bedroom and put his hands precisely on his knees, in the prescribed manner to show his good intentions. Now there were sounds from the kitchen —Hao was talking to the old woman, and Jasmine had interrupted, asking something in a sharp, frightened voice. Durell turned the iron key in the door lock.

"Very good," Shan said. "What we have to say had best be kept between ourselves for now."

"Did Colonel Chu lie? He said he had killed you."

"He thought he had. He was a bit careless. Indeed, I was close to death. On my body, you will find scars that you do not have, of course. But I was saved."

"How?"

"I do not know whose men they were. They found me floating in the Tanshui River, in Taipei." Shan began to tremble, and he said apologetically, "Forgive me, I am very hungry, and I smell the food in the kitchen. The body betrays us all, it seems. I have not eaten for three days, except for what I could steal; not much was available to a thief."

"Who knows you are here?"

"No one."

"You haven't reported to the Black House?"

"No, but I gave the young lady the maps of the tunnels to help you escape."

"Jasmine knew of you when she came for me?"

"Did she not tell you?" Shan asked curiously. "It is strange. Is she not your companion, your partner?"

"She's supposed to be. I'm not so sure."

Shan nodded quietly. There was something about him that Durell liked—and he reflected dourly that perhaps it was because the man was such an intimate duplicate of himself. He put aside the knife, aware of Shan's eyes reflecting relief.

"You'll eat when the rest of us do—when you've explained yourself. Who pulled you out of the Tanshui River?"

"I did not know them. Americans, of course. Agents, I'm sure, from K Section. They were not Haystead's men, or I'd have been left for dead again. Neither, of course, were they Chu's people from the Zebra outfit. I can only conclude they were from your own agency."

Durell hid his puzzlement. McFee had said nothing about the fact that Shan was alive. But McFee must have known this. He felt a deeper confusion than he had ever known before. The shock of facing his duplicate, this man that he had been fashioned to represent, still vibrated in him. He had studied Shan's dossier, he knew this man to be a brilliant agent of the Black House. But the real Shan now sat here, quiet-spoken, hungry, obviously weak from injuries, speaking as a friend. It made no sense. The dim pattern he had begun to perceive vanished like a cobweb blown away by a sudden gust of wind. But he allowed none of his perplexity to show, and the real Major Shan smiled approval.

"Yes, you are very good, Cajun. Much better than we, of the Black House, had supposed you to be."

"How did you get here?" Durell demanded. "If you lie to me, I'll know it. If you're here to take me back to the Black House, forget it. If you have others outside the temple, then your mission is one of suicide, because you'll die first."

"I understand." Shan coughed and winced with inner pain. "And you must understand, too. We are both in a most difficult situation. My danger is no less than yours. I could not convince anyone that your acts in the Black House were not mine."

"That's true."

"So, frankly, you have forfeited my life by taking my place and acting as a traitor to my beloved China. Yes, I love my country, as you love yours, and my people's welfare and safety are all that concern me. But you have made me a dead man in my motherland. When I returned and heard, through my own sources, that a 'Major Shan' had done this and that, I knew it would be suicidal to show myself and attempt to explain." Shan shrugged. "I did not really believe it possible for another man to be molded so exactly in my own image. It is uncanny. I find it difficult to accept, seeing you, and I am sure you feel the same way. But you have an advantage. You look like Shan, but underneath, I know you are Sam Durell, from K Section, an American, and if you are successful, you will once again be shaped to look like yourself. For me, there is no hope of escaping the consequences of what has been done to us by our superiors. We are victims of the work we do, obedient to orders and dedicated to—what?" Shan spread his hands. "In the end, we will die and be forgotten, except in some dusty file marked 'Secret—Classified —Closed.' "

"You are philosophical, for someone in our business," Durell observed.

"It helps one to survive. To an intelligent man, our vocation would be difficult to accept without an inner conviction as to the rightness of things."

"Do you think an atomic war would be right?"

"Of course not. I work for peace." Shan's smile made his mouth dip at the corners. "It is an ambiguity, is it not, that men such as we deal in dark violence, to preserve the world?"

"Do you know of the Six Sentinels?" Durell asked sharply.

"I do. They were my assignment, just as they are yours."

"In what way?"

"To learn who these men are, and who their counterparts are in China. It is a silent, tacit conspiracy between these two groups to provoke nuclear warfare between our nations. The irony of it is that both groups are certain that they, and only they, will be the victors in such a showdown. But to my mind, everyone in the human race will be the losers if this happens."

"What did you learn of the Six Sentinels?"

"Not much." Shan was rueful. "My mission was rudely interrupted by your Colonel Chu."

"He's not on my side," Durell said flatly. "He's working with you."

"No. Only for himself, that man. He should be killed."

"He may already have been," Durell said grimly. "Now tell me how you got here, and what you expect to do."

"May I—may I have something to eat first?"

"No."

"You do not trust me?"

"Should I?"

"I suppose not. Well, a stomach that has been empty as long as mine can wait a bit longer. When I was pulled out of the Tanshui River by what I think were K Section men, I was almost dead, of course. This was more that five weeks ago—and in the course of that time, you went through your transformation to duplicate me." Shan shook his head in wonder. "I was badly injured. Chu left me for dead. I was certainly more dead than alive. I do not remember where I was taken and nursed back to a reasonable facsimile of health. You need not fear me, Cajun. I am invalided. You could knock me down with the back of your hand. And I fear I may be more of a liability than an asset."

"How so?"

The Chinese said flatly: "Why, you and I must work together, somehow. We both have the same goal, to uncover the identities of the Six Sentinels and stop their scheme to provoke nuclear war. Is that not so?"

"Perhaps."

"Then, in any case, I remember very little. My medical care was excellent, but until a week ago, I was too ill to do much. Then I was flown here, three days ago, in a Lotus plane. The men who took me were anonymous. They said very little. They only told me you had taken my place in China and that if I had any hope of living, I must find you and join you. They said you would know what to do. I'm not sure, now, since my appearance is such a surprise to you. In any case, we both share the same leaky boat, eh? We must bail it out together, or drown."

"How do you propose any advantage out of this?"

"We have one great asset," said Shan. "We are identical."

Durell nodded. "Yes, I think the fact that I am really two men, in a sense, can get us out of China and back to Taiwan."

"You mean to go back there?"

"I mean to find the head of the Sentinel conspiracy and kill or expose him."

Shan was silent. He kneaded his hands together, pushed back his thick black hair, and sighed. "I have every reason to believe, Durell, that the true conspirator at the head of it all is your own chief, General McFee."

Sixteen

THE OLD WOMAN BEGAN TO SERVE FOOD IN THE kitchen. It was late in the afternoon now, and the rain had settled into a steady downpour. Dusk came early. While the real Shan wolfed down the pork and steamed bread the old woman handed him, Durell followed Hao's gesture and climbed an old, polished bamboo ladder to the top attic of the Buddhist temple. From here there was an unexpected view, through a slit in the rafters, of a nearby boulevard where thousands of marchers still persisted in their celebration. There were acrobats, peasants, dancers, choruses, all with bands and floats, flowers and pennants, animal figures and dragons, lions and tigers, as well as the ubiquitous Chinese cymbals. Hao shut the trapdoor in the attic room. It was cool and damp here, above the incense burners and the chanting monks below.

"I am sorry I had to surprise you. You can imagine my shock when Major Shan appeared. He knew of this place and all my activities, for many months, he said. It was information he kept to himself, while he worked on his mission, in order to keep me under personal surveillance." The little monk clasped his hands together. "For a moment, of course, I thought he was you. But he was very weak—he has a limp, even yet—and he behaved reasonably, wishing only to meet and confer with you."

"You did the right thing," Durell said.

"What will you do with him?" Hao asked anxiously.

"We'll use him," Durell said. "He's willing to cooperate. Not every enemy agent," he added with a small smile, "is a monster."

"True, Shan seems to be a reasonable man."

"And a dangerous one."

Hao paused nervously. "Jasmine told me that she gave you the transmitter pen—the Zebra microminiaturized transmitter."

"That's right."

"Have you examined it?"

"How many do you have?"

"Originally, we received six. Their range is most extraordinary." Hao smiled thinly. "Under Heaven's Eye, man seems to work miracles. Let Heaven see to it that these miracles are used beneficently."

"I think it's up to us to see to that," Durell said.

In the shadows of the temple attic, he took the pen that Jasmine had given him and examined it curiously. He knew enough about electronics to appreciate the infinitely detailed workings of the device when he unscrewed it and drew out the tiny cylinder of microscopic circuitry, together with a power source he could not analyze. Like the strides taken in space photography, detection mikes had developed far beyond the point known in the public mind. Except for a slight overweight, the pen looked utterly innocent when closed up.

"How much range does this have?" he asked the monk.

"I have never tested it fully. We planted three of these and three other forms with officials in the government hierarchy. Each has a different frequency and is monitored on recording tape hidden in the apartment downstairs. At regular intervals, these are sent off to Zebra headquarters in Taiwan."

"How do you get them back?"

"By airplane pickup, north of here. The courier is due in four days. Do you plan to leave with Shan?"

"I must. I'll take Shan with me."

"Do you trust him, sir?"

"No," Durell said. "Can you make a transmission to the courier and to Taiwan directly?"

"I have contacted the courier twice, in emergencies—when two previous K Section men came here and failed. It was necessary to report their capture and execution."

Durell handed him the pencil. "Can you do so again, with this?"

"It will be dangerous. Others besides Shan may now be aware of my activities." The little monk was apologetic. "My life is in Buddha's blessed hands; but the cause for which I have labored, often against my conscience for China, must not fail. Peace for all men is my goal, my dear sir. I will try to contact the courier."

"Good. Tell him there will be three of us, then—two men and Jasmine."

"Yes. As for the woman——" Hao coughed again. "She is most devoted to you, sir. She has been waiting——"

"All right," Durell said. "Make the transmission as soon as you can."

There was a distant popping of firecrackers on the boulevard as evening fell, and once a party of young schoolgirls invaded the temple courtyard, carrying with them fluttering scarves which they used for dancing. Everyone in the apartment kept silent until the small flood of celebrants was gone and the quiet bells and intonations of the priests resumed. A few lanterns were lit in the courtyard as night came.

Hao did not come down from the attic with Durell, but Jasmine was waiting for him. Her eyes anxiously searched his face.

"Shan is asleep. The man was badly injured." Her voice was uncertain. "Can't I do something for your face,

Sam? Let me help you. I know you're in pain and won't admit it——"

He nodded. His head throbbed, and all his facial bones ached. He was aware of deep exhaustion, compounded by the questions that remained unanswered in the back of his mind. He gave himself into Jasmine's hands, and she led him into a deserted area of the temple, pushed him down on some cloth bales, and then returned for a pan of hot water and aspirin, and a tube of ointment which she applied to his worst bruises.

"I don't think I'll ever adjust to it," she whispered. "I know you are my own Sam, and I love you—but you and Major Shan are identical, both of you more Chinese than I, really——"

"Take it easy, Jasmine," he said.

She said pleadingly, "Just, please—trust me." She paused. "I don't want your gratitude. Haven't I done all you expected of me? Don't you know I'd give my life for you?"

"McFee sent you to spy on me. Why?"

"Is that so unusual, in something like this?"

"He always trusted me before," Durell said.

"This—this one is different. He's in terrible danger himself. K Section is in danger. Surely you know that now. If McFee loses, he'll be killed—oh, not obviously murdered, but in an auto accident or something like that. He's fighting shadows, just like you, and can't trust anyone—just like you."

Durell said grimly, "Both Chu and Shan said he's one of the Sentinels."

"Can you believe that?"

"I don't know what to believe. I'll know better, when we get back to Taiwan and find some facts."

"What will you do if the evidence—which may be false —shows that McFee is a traitor?" she asked.

"I don't know yet."

"But I know you, Sam. There is no room for compromise in you. I'm afraid for you. I'm afraid of what they —whoever they are—may make you do. If you don't survive, then my life—my life means nothing."

He was aware of the warm, salty slide of tears on her cheeks as she pressed her face to his. Her mouth sought his hungrily. Her rich body was warm as she eased back upon him as they lay in the gloom, upon the bales of cloth. The storeroom smelled of incense and old spices. Dimly, he heard the sound of muted gongs again. He thought that it was good to be here for these moments, alone with her, apart from the dangers in the vast city around them. For these few minutes, he felt safe, and the imminent threat of sudden death with which he lived faded into the background.

He rolled over in the dusk and took her gently, while the temple gongs made the air vibrate softly with their strange melodies.

Seventeen

Major shan was much improved in the morning. Peking was back to normal, with the streetsweepers cleaning up the debris of paper flowers and festoons of wet banners. The rain had stopped briefly, and the air was a pale, washed blue, crisp with the tokens of coming winter. Durell had slept fitfully, and he remembered vague half-dreams in which he found himself helplessly trapped. He awoke to find his duplicate image staring at him over a cup of steaming tea. Another tray of breakfast tea and rice and delicately smoked fish rested beside his cot.

He looked for Jasmine, but she was gone.

"Where is the girl?"

Shan was admiring. "I like the way you wake up, sir. In full possession of every faculty. The girl is with Hao. They are using the radio, carefully, trying to contact the courier. Do you truly mean to fly back to Taiwan?"

"There's nothing more for me to do here. Chien Y-Wu is dead. He can't talk now, at any rate, and that part of the scheme to give China an excuse to attack the Nationalists is ended."

"But the conspiracy in your country still exists, as it does in mine," Shan pointed out. "I see that is why you must return. But our lives are forfeited, both here and there."

"They always have been," Durell said flatly. "But do we just roll over and die?"

"Neither of us is made that way. I had hoped your mind would be open, when I came to you, and that you could accept my help as a temporary ally. I am pleased you will take me to Taiwan with you." The Chinese touched his face and smiled. "Perhaps you can think of some advantage in our looking so identical. Confusion to our enemies, eh? How do you say it? Now you see it, now you don't! We can be in two places at once."

Durell reached for the pot of hot green tea and swallowed the steaming liquid gratefully. He would have preferred bourbon, or the chicory-flavored Louisiana coffee he was addicted to. He was suddenly hungry and ate the fish and steamed bun of bread with relish. "Do you really want to go back to Taiwan with me?"

"I think I must. I had to make sure you were here, in my place, and working on the same mission. Unless I can prove myself, the Black House will hunt me down and kill me. I'm a renegade, you see, and like you, have no choice." The Chinese spread his hands. "I want to work together with you. I will trust you until we die or win our way out of this dilemma."

Durell thought about it, and then began talking of various ways in which they could make use of their identical looks. The Chinese listened with quiet care and nodded agreement.

Hao said there was nothing in the newspapers or on the radio about an escaped imperialist agent from the Black House. Durell hadn't expected any announcement, but he had no illusions about how the Black House would be scouring Peking for him at this moment, searching trains, planes, and bullock carts in a desperate hunt for "Major Shan."

The day passed quietly. The old woman brought some salve for the bruises on Durell's face, and he asked Jasmine for a cosmetic to hide the black-and-blue marks. He noted, with some dismay, that his skin was losing its yellowish-brown cast. The effect of Ike Greentree's pigmentation treatments for changing his complexion was not lasting as long as he'd hoped. Almost two weeks were gone. He had a week left. Toward noon of that day, Hao went out to obtain some uniforms he said he could get. He promised to be back in an hour, but by nightfall the monk had not returned, and there was no way of learning what had happened to him.

After the evening meal the old woman vanished, too.

With darkness, Durell noted that the gongs and chanting in the temple had ended, and he went there. The priests and the acolytes were gone. The temple was dark.

He was alone with Jasmine and Major Shan.

By midnight no one had come back. It began to rain again, a sullen downpour that did nothing to lift their morale. Durell felt trapped. He went into the temple attic room and considered the transmitters; he began to take the room apart, inch by inch. Shan and Jasmine joined him there.

"You will not find it, Cajun," Shan said quietly. "Hao probably memorized everything."

"I hope not."

Jasmine said, "What are we searching for?"

"Hao's code book," Durell said. "He was to send a message to the Lotus courier and the plane that can take us back. Every minute we stay here adds to our risk of being caught by the Black House people. They won't show us much mercy."

"What has happened to Hao?" she asked.

Durell exchanged a glance with Shan. "Odds are, Tai Ma nabbed him, and he's being questioned now."

"Perhaps he will not talk," Shan said. "Hao is a very strong man, with his faith to support him—perhaps a stronger faith than my own Communism or your patriotism, Cajun."

"Even if he dies in silence," Durell said, "they'll identify him, sooner or later, and trace their way here. Why do you think the old woman and priests have disappeared? It's only a matter of time. We must leave, but we must have Hao's code book first."

Shan said, "I do not believe it exists. But we will search, of course. One must try, eh?"

It was strange to work next to his mirror-image as they tore the storeroom apart and examined the transmitters and the Zebra device. Durell's knowledge of electronics, gleaned during many tedious hours at K Section's "Farm" in the Maryland countryside, soon solved the riddle of the microminiaturized pen transmitter. But he did not know frequency or code, or the landing field used by the Lotus courier. Even if they should be wildly lucky and get out of Peking and find the plane, he thought grimly, they might still run into treachery.

An hour went by. And another. Shan used almost the identical search techniques Durell had been accustomed to use himself. At two o'clock in the morning Durell was ready to give up. Shan had found a cigarette somewhere, and smoked it quietly while he considered the room, trying to think of another place to search. It was then that Jasmine, who had watched helplessly, stood up.

"The books!" she exclaimed.

Durell turned his head. "What books?"

"Hao collected old Buddhist scrolls. He told me about them while you were watching the Black House to locate Tai Ma. He was very proud of the collection."

"Did he show them to you?"

"Yes, they're in a temple room, behind the silk screens."

The rain had grown heavier and colder. In the late-hour gloom, the courtyard looked desolate. They ran across into the temple proper. A cat scampered out of their way, and they all halted, breathing lightly and quickly. From the wide street outside came the sudden sound of a motorcar. It was unusual enough in Peking's streets to freeze them again. The motor sound was then drowned out by the melodic clanging of one of Peking's ubiquitous trolley buses going by. When it passed, Durell could no longer hear the engine noise of the car.

"It's stopped," he whispered.

He moved deeper into the shadows of the yellow-painted temple portico. It was difficult to see through the rain and the darkness. Jasmine shivered against him. Then he heard the tramp of military boots, a soft command, and lights flickered from several hand torches as the street gate was opened. Shan drew a long, soft breath. No one moved.

The dim shapes of half a dozen men strode in. Faint light reflected from the gleaming metal of their automatic rifles. They moved at a dogtrot to posts about the courtyard while two officers, with flashlights, made for the apartment. Durell wondered what traces of their occupancy there might be found. He couldn't think of anything. The food dishes had been cleaned and stowed up; the pallets on which they had slept were not in themselves incriminating. But he could not remember what Jasmine had done with the medicating salves for his face. He turned his head very slowly to look at her as they stood motionless in the shadows of the portico. He could barely see her face, although she was less than an arm's length away.

The officers were in the apartment for what seemed an interminable time. When they came out, their stride was not hurried, and Durell was relieved; they had found nothing suspicious.

One of the soldiers hawked and coughed and spat. His nearest companion reprimanded him.

"Sacred building?" the first jeered. "You must get rid of such revisionist sentiments, Comrade. It's all capitalist garbage, meant to keep the people in ignorance. This place should be burned down, or turned into a school for our children!"

The two officers started directly for the temple steps where Durell stood. He held his breath as their flashlights danced curiously over the wet, painted timbers and the tiled, dripping roof. There was a leak in the eaves, and the heavy rain had started a solid sheet of water pouring down over the steps, directly in the officers' path. At the same time, the second soldier at the gate responded with an angry argument to the one who had coughed and spat. The two officers hesitated, then turned away to calm an incipient fight.

Durell and Shan and Jasmine did not move. There was more conversation at the gate, while the rain came down heavier. The soldiers grumbled. At last the two officers doused their flashlights and the little squad, in their blue uniforms, formed ragged ranks and marched away.

They left the gate open.

In the dark emptiness of the temple sanctuary, Jasmine found a small candle. The gongs and cymbals gleamed on their brass stands. They followed the girl silently through the shadows as she led them into a small room hidden beyond the gleaming, ruby-eyed statue of a gently smiling Buddha. Against the walls were square teak pigeonholes containing silk-wrapped scrolls with jeweled handles and scarlet tassels.

"Hao showed these to me." Jasmine looked helpless. "But there are hundreds, and I don't know where to start."

"Did Hao show you any in particular?" Durell asked.

"These over here. Just one or two. They didn't mean much, except for their beautiful calligraphy."

"Maybe he was trying to lead us here by telling you of this, in case he met with trouble."

It was after three in the morning when Durell and Shan started examining the scrolls, and he posted Jasmine at the door in case the militia returned. By four o'clock they'd had no luck. At five, his eyes blurred from scanning the ancient parchment scripts. Durell's Mandarin was not quite up to translating all of the finely brushed characters, and Shan did almost double his amount. There was a faint gray light of dawn when Durell pulled another scroll out and unrolled it—to find several sheets of rice-paper, obviously new in contrast to the yellowed parchment.

"Here it is," he murmured.

Shan came quickly to his side. "Yes, it's Hao's code for contacting your Zebra people. Of course, I know that Haystead's E Branch of the NSA initiated the entire Zebra and Lotus operations. It was not difficult," the Chinese smiled, "to discover that the I.P.S. Electronics Company in Taipei, where Haystead makes his headquarters, is simply a front for your NSA's electronic warfare. I tried to penetrate the I.P.S., but I failed—the signal alarms beat me—and that was when Colonel Chu trapped me."

"Let me see the code," Durell said.

Shan handed him the rice paper. "Now all we need do is broadcast for help. We run the risk of detection, with the Black House as alert for you as they must be."

"They don't know there are two of us," Durell said. "I'll give the transmitter a whirl now, before Hao, the poor little devil, breaks down and talks. If he does, then everything hits the proverbial fan."

Eighteen

IT RAINED ALL DAY, THE ROOF DRAINS OVERFLOWED, the streets gurgled with water, and there were several inches of water in the temple courtyard. The militia did not return, and Durell wondered if little Hao were alive or dead.

Durell kept the tiny transmitter going at regular intervals during that dark afternoon. An hour after he told Shan his plan, Shan left the temple grounds like a gray shadow, and was gone for a long time. He came back as silently and suddenly as he had vanished. His black almond eyes twinkled.

"I let a militiaman see me at Peihai Park. He was easy to escape, but there is a general alert out. The story given out publicly is that the militia must be armed to repel imperialist aggressors from across the Yalu." Shan laughed softly. "I made sure the militiaman saw me, so it would be reported that I was wandering in the rain in the northeast area of Peking. Here."

The Chinese handed Durell a long-barreled Russian machine pistol. It was heavy and bulky, but Durell felt better immediately. The magazine was loaded, and he thrust it into his waistband. "And you, Shan?"

"Next trip. Anything on the radio?"

"No response yet."

At dusk Shan went out again and was gone longer this time, almost two hours, and it was totally dark when he reappeared.

"I went to Peking Central Station," he reported, grinning. "One of the regime's showplaces, eh? I tried to buy a ticket back to Wuhan. I was spotted at once, as I wished to be."

"You're taking big chances," Jasmine said tightly.

Shan looked at her with a new expression veiled in his black eyes. "It is my city, of course. I was brought up here, except when the Japanese came when I was a boy and I left with Mao Tse-tung and his Communist cadres for the Long March. As an urchin under the old regime, I learned every alley and corner of Peking. You see, I was a thief."

Jasmine was interested. "It sounds like the way I was brought up in San Francisco."

"I have never met an American Chinese, Jasmine."

"Maybe you're lucky," she said wryly. "You haven't seen my dossier, have you?"

"I know about you," Shan said gently.

"Women with my past have been swept off Peking's streets like so much garbage," Jasmine said bitterly.

"Don't be ashamed," Shan said, "of what the capitalist imperialists made of your childhood, or of what you were forced to do as a young girl to keep body and soul together."

"It doesn't bother your Communist morality?"

"One deals with the facts of the present, and in hope for the future." Shan looked at the girl for a long moment, and again something stirred in his long eyes. "In

Peihai Park there is a white Buddhist dagoba, very unique. The people joke about it and call it the 'Peppermint Bottle.' I would like one day to show it to you."

"I doubt if that time will ever come, Shan." Jasmine's voice was soft. "But it is a nice thought to keep."

Shan had returned with two militia uniforms and two more guns. The largest, with its thin quilting, fitted Durell reasonably well. Jasmine's was too large, but she pulled and pinned and adjusted it to suit.

Shan said abruptly, "Do you love Sam, Jasmine?"

She considered him. "Yes, I do."

"But he is like a Chinese."

"I know what he really looks like," she said.

"But now he looks like me," Shan pointed out.

"Yes. Exactly like you."

On his next trip, which lasted only an hour, Shan reported going to the celebrated Fan Shan restaurant and enjoying a dinner reflecting the same menus enjoyed by the last Dowager Empress. He brought some of the food back with him.

"The waitress recognized me; she was a Black House agent I had once worked with. I saw her go to the telephone, and by now Tai Ma is properly confused. He thinks his men are reporting you, not me, and it keeps this place safe for a time while you use the radio."

"I haven't raised anything yet," Durell admitted. He had not stopped poring over the monk Hao's code books by the light of the guttering candle.

"When I left the restaurant," Shan went on, "I took a bus to the Great People's Hall. It is a truly magnificient place, bright with chandeliers, busy with correspondents and photographers. I made sure I appeared in several news photos being taken of visiting dignitaries from Africa, attending the State banquet." Shan grinned and looked almost boyish. "No, the People's Hall is not truly magnificent, except in size. Its taste is execrable. Metallic columns with iridescent glitter and most conventional designs. Chou En-lai himself was there, with a thousand bureaucrats. The man has charm, but he is rather saturnine, don't you think? One never really knows what goes on in his brain. Did you know he prefers Western symphonies? He endured one of our traditional pieces—the three-stringed fiddles and our *chang,* the mouth organ; but he truly applauded Brahms."

Shan had brought a bottle of fiery North China wine, which they shared while Durell kept broadcasting. Once he thought he heard an uncertain response; but the dim voice faded away almost instantly. He kept at that frequency, murmuring into the tiny transmitter, using the emergency code words that demanded a prompt reply. But nothing more happened.

With Shan's help, they were now all armed and in militia uniform. With Shan's popping up everywhere in Peking, the Black House would not be likely to return to search the temple hideout. Durell was aware of Shan and Jasmine murmuring quietly together as he continued with the radio. His voice had gone hoarse, and exhaustion dragged at his nerves and mind. He was thinking of McFee, hardly aware of his companions, when he heard a whispering:

"Zebra Twenty-six, Lotus Two. Zebra Twenty-six——"

Tht words faded. Desperately, he turned the tiny adjustment dial. Infinitesimal cracklings were his response. He turned it the other way.

"——Lotus Two, come in, I hear you——"

The Chinese voice was precise. "This is Zebra——"

"Lotus Two," Durell said quietly. "I read you clear."

"Good. This is not an authorized transmission time——"

"I have a Mayday signal for you."

"Very well. Transmit, please."

"We need the Zebra courier in twenty-four hours. It is urgent. Top priority. Can you do it? Can you do it?"

"Can try, Lotus Two. The usual coordinates?"

"Give them to me, please, Zebra."

There was a moment's silence. "It is not in the regulations to transmit——"

"I told you, Mayday." Durrell spoke urgently and hoped the distant Zebra man recognized his conviction. "We need help. Give me the coordinates."

The Chinese voice went cold. "You are not Lotus Two, are you?"

"No. This is Shan."

Another silence. "Understood. Where is Lotus Two?"

"Gone. Perhaps permanently."

"Just a minute."

The tiny receiver crackled, then went dead. Durell stared at the tiny mechanism in his hand. Surely, he thought, somewhere in Peking they were being monitored, vectors and intersecting coordinates being calculated. Then——

"Lotus Two, this is Zebra Twenty-six. Here are the coordinates for one nine hundred hours on Three-Ten. Are you ready?"

A brief list of numerals followed, intoned with a mechanical precision. Durell asked for a repeat, received it, and said, "Roger, Lotus Two. Out. And thank you."

"Please be prompt. The safety factor allows only eight minutes at rendezvous."

"We'll be there. There are three of us."

"But——"

"Three passengers for Zebra headquarters," he said firmly. "Out."

He clicked off the microtransmitter and turned to Shan and Jasmine. They stared at him as if he were a stranger.

"Let's get out of here," he said.

The rain was a help, thickening the darkness. According to the coordinates, the landing field used by Lotus planes was almost two hundred miles north of Peking, in the direction of Chengteh. They would have to go through the Great Wall of China, that ancient guardian barrier erected in the Ch'in dynasty by Shih Hwang-ti in the third century B.C.. Running 1500 miles from Kansu to Chinwangtao, in Hopeh province, along the southern edge of the Mongolian plain, it was built in the east of earth and stone, faced with brick, and was pierced at regular intervals with "Grand Stations," gates and watch towers added by the Mings over five centuries ago. It would be a difficult point to cross, Durell estimated, even in this day.

The Peking University professor, Jen Feng-Bao, met them at dawn in his battered but precious Warszawa. When they scrambled in, outside the temple gate, the scholarly little man picked up speed at once.

"Have you heard anything of my friend Hao?" he asked.

"We think the Black House has him," Durell said.

"Then he will die, because he will not talk."

"How far can you take us?"

"Just outside the city. We would be noticed if I went farther. I have train tickets for you to Chengteh. But you must get off at the first village after Amyang. Do you know where to go from there?" Durell nodded, and Jen went on: "There is a farmer there—he was once a great landowner, but he obtained a new identity years ago— who will meet you in a cart on the western road from the rail station. He will take you to the rendezvous." The professor smiled thinly. "I wish you luck."

"Will you be safe?" Jasmine asked.

"I put my trust in Hao's silence, as we all must."

A westerly wind, bringing the first wintry gale from the Gobi, had changed the tempo of life in Peking. The red and yellow leaves were battered from the trees, and the air smelled of coal smoke from the stoves in the low, walled houses. A few trucks passed by, carrying apples and brilliantly orange persimmons. Most of the provision traffic into Peking consisted of carts pulled by donkeys, horses, or oxen, and even some hauled by the peasants themselves. The Warszawa threaded carefully through this dawn traffic. Jasmine looked longingly at the warm padded pants and quilted jackets the farmers wore, but for the hour's trip in the gray, wet dawn, they were all silent.

At a small center where vegetable stands were being set up, filled with cabbages and carrots, sweet potatoes and beans, the car halted, and Jen said reluctantly, "It is as far as I can go. The rail station is just that way. I wish you good luck. The train should be in within twenty minutes."

"You've been a big help," Durell said.

Jen looked from him to Shan, and shook his head. "I do not know how this was done, but it is remarkable. I do not know your purpose, but I trust it will be for the good of the people and my students."

"We hope it will be," said Shan.

The train was on time. Shan boarded at one end, Durell and Jasmine at the other. There were militiamen in the coaches, but thanks to Shan's many appearances in the city, the search was being concentrated within Peking—at least for the time.

There were the usual propaganda speakers on the train's system, the dust-women and tea service, which they accepted gratefully. The train was overheated, and their wet clothing steamed. In their militia uniforms, they were accepted without another glance as the train rumbled north through a drowning countryside. Veils of mist drifted across the fields and hills, and occasional solid fog blotted out the landscape entirely. At the third stop, a village crowded with troops and peasants, they bought rice, tea, and smoked fish for breakfast. Shan had provided them with currency to pay their way. Durell looked for his duplicate on the train platform, but did not see him, and credited Shan with keeping out of sight so they wouldn't be noticed together.

After two hours, the train lurched to a halt. They seemed to be in the middle of nowhere. The countryside looked desolate. Newly planted copses of trees were shrouded by rain. Water ran across the tracks. After a few moments, the train started again and eased carefully across a trestle, with the rails out of sight under the running water of a flooded stream.

"Do we have enough time?" Jasmine murmured anxiously.

"Six hours on the train," Durell said. "I've allowed two more to get to the airfield. We don't have to arrive until seven this evening. It should be dark then, and safe enough."

The delays due to flooding were an unexpected factor. There were two more halts, one in the middle of a drowned plain of water that reached invisibly through the mist. The last delay was for almost an hour, and Durell bought a newspaper from one of the women attendants and pretended to read it with Jasmine, as militiamen restlessly wandered up and down the coaches. Once, a stout, moon-faced lance-corporal stopped and stared at Durell, his small black eyes puzzled. He looked as if he were about to say something, scratched his head, and stared back at the rear coaches, obviously remembering he had seen Shan. But he only shrugged and went on.

The rain persisted. At noon, they reached the checkpoint at the Great Wall. The delay here was longer. The militia detrained, and Durell and Jasmine also got off into the cold mist at the base of the towering old bastion. There were regular army troops here, along the wooden platform that ran through the tunnel in the Great Wall. Army jeeps of Chinese manufacture, some field guns, and truckloads of more troops had collected here, where a small village had sprung up of modern, barrack-like buildings. Durell and Jasmine walked along as if part of the militia company. He did not see Shan. There was an argument between the militia officer and an army captain. The captain demanded something, and the militiaman resisted complying. The delay seemed interminable. The militia settled down under sheds along the tracks to eat, and in the middle of it, Shan appeared, walked up to the disputing officers, and said something to them. Both men stared at him resentfully. Shan exhibited some cards and papers, and there was a prompt lowering of voices and then the army captain, with his red shoulder tabs sagging on his sopping, quilted coat, turned away.

There was waving and shouting and everyone boarded the train again. In ten minutes they were through the Great Wall.

There were two more halts because of flooding. Darkness fell, and a few lights shone in the countryside. Time was running out, Durell thought. At last the small station of Amyang appeared. The militia debarked, and the train was almost empty to the next village, where Durell and

Jasmine got off on the small, sodden platform. The stationhouse was the only light to be seen. He and Jasmine moved off into the muddy village street and waited beside a low wall for Shan to appear. The train rumbled off. Durell began to swear under his breath. Jasmine stood close to him, deep concern on her pale, tired face.

"Where is Shan?" Her teeth chattered. "He's not bad, you know. He—he reminds me a bit of you, Sam."

"So I noticed."

"I—I'm all mixed up. I wish I'd never accepted this job——"

Durell straightened. "There he is."

Looming out of the dark village street came a creaking bullock cart with a peasant in a wide conical straw hat and a poncho-like quilted cape. Beside him was Shan. The bullock lumbered to a halt and Shan waved them up on the tail gate. The rain beat at them, but Shan's teeth gleamed in a wide smile.

"This man expected us. But he says it may be difficult to get to his field in time. There are floods, of course."

"Won't it be too muddy for the Lotus plane to land?" Jasmine asked.

"It's crushed rock, an old Japanese airstrip that everyone seems to have forgotten. But we've got to hurry."

Durell said, "How did you get us through the Wall?"

"You forget, Cajun, I'm a Black House agent. I have enough identity cards to prove anything. I showed the army man enough to convince him he would be shot as an enemy of the people if he didn't order the train on at once."

The peasant was a hunched, anonymous blot of darkness behind his huge bullock. The village was quickly swallowed in the evening gloom. The station lights vanished behind them. Durell was silent, wondering about Shan's motives. It could all be a trap to capture one of the Lotus planes, he thought, with Shan deceiving them until the last moment. For a time, he considered using his militiaman's automatic and making Shan and the peasant his prisoners. But that might be awkward. In this desolate countryside he might never find the airstrip.

The bullock plodded down the road at an agonizingly slow pace. The beast could not be hurried, and the Chinese farmer made no attempt to do so. The wind blew in their faces, pelting them with the cold rain.

"What time is it?" Jasmine whispered.

Shan said, "It is eighteen-thirty hours. Thirty minutes to the rendezvous—if the plane can make it."

"Can *we* make it?" Jasmine asked.

Shan shrugged. "We do the best we can."

They passed a lighted farmhouse, then for a long time they lumbered on without a gleam of light anywhere on the horizon. The bullock kept to the country lane by habit; without the beast's guidance, they would have been lost in minutes. Time passed. They entered a stretch of dark woods, and the bullock halted, head lowered, horns swinging from side to side. The peasant spat and got down from his seat. Durell joined him. A tree had fallen across the road, massive enough to defy their efforts to move it, at first. For five precious minutes they struggled and heaved to remove the tangled growth. There was no way to get the cart around it through the thick brush. At last, panting and sweating despite the cold wind, Shan said, "We must walk the rest of the way."

"How far?" Durell asked.

"Two miles. Perhaps three."

They left the peasant and his cart and struck off in the darkness. Shan had obtained a flashlight from the peasant, and they managed to keep to the road without getting lost in the woods. Leaves swirled and fell about their shoulders. There were two more windfalls from the storm, and then they came out of the woods into dark fields. A dim light shone to the right.

"That way," Shan said.

"You know this place, Shan?" Durell asked.

"Yes, I landed here with the Americans who saved my life and shipped me back to help you. I promised them I would do what I could do for you, and that is all."

"Do they expect you back?"

"I do not know."

"You'll be imprisoned as a spy," Durell said. "And if the Kuomintang get you on Taiwan, you'll be shot."

"I must take that chance and do what I think is right. I understand our alliance is temporary. Do you not have a fable in your land, about a man without a country? In some ways, I have made myself an exile, too. I do not know what the future will bring me. Perhaps I may never be able to return to China. In that case—" Shan shrugged expressively and hunched his head as the wind pelted them. "I think we are here."

A dilapidated farmhouse compound showed up through the darkness. No lights shone in the front windows. Durell put his arm around Jasmine as she sagged against the wall. Beyond the farmhouse was a dimly visible field that was lost in the blowing curtains of rain. Shan vanished inside for some minutes, then came back with a handful of flares, which he distributed to Durell and Jasmine. "I remember we had these to guide the Lotus pilot when I was brought here."

They worked desperately against the fleeting minutes to light up the narrow strip. It was already time for the plane to appear, but there was no sound in the lowering sky except for the moan of the wind and the pelting rain. The red flares spat their brief glow into the night and seemed abnormally bright against the darkness. In a few minutes, the job was done and they gathered at the end of the strip nearest the farmhouse.

A minute passed. Another. Shan kept looking at his watch. The rendezvous time had gone by. Durell watched the dark sky and waited. Once he thought he heard a faint drone, but then it faded. Visibility was limited to only a few hundred feet. One of the flares was used up and guttered out, and then another died a moment later.

Jasmine clutched at his arm. "Listen!"

He heard it at the same moment. It was the sound of an engine, with faint, echoing overtones. Puzzled, he turned to Shan. He understood what it was, too.

"A truck is coming," Durell said.

"Yes. And the plane, too."

"A truck?" Jasmine asked.

"Maybe police, or troops. Maybe the peasant was found and questioned. We shall see, Jasmine." Shan smiled and took her arm. "You must not be afraid, whatever happens."

"I'm not, but—yes, I am. I probably don't belong in this business. Neither do you, Shan. You're not really like Durell, after all. Durell lets nothing stop him. Nothing can sway him. But you—you've risked everything in your life——"

The appearance of the plane broke into her words. It swooped and drifted over the field like a wide-winged dragonfly of monstrous proportions, its extraordinarily long wings vibrating as the pilot banked, vanished, and then came back with landing lights glowing like brilliant jeweled shafts through the teeming rain. Durell listened to the sound of the approaching truck at the same time. It was about a mile off. He turned as the Lotus pilot came in, touched down, bounced, touched again. The wind made the port wing come down and almost scrape the ground. The aircraft teetered, bounced once more, and then taxied in, flooding them with its landing beams. The lights went off in another moment, and the Lotus stopped. A hatch opened, and Durell took Jasmine's hand and they ran for it.

Three minutes later, they lifted off the airfield as the approaching truck's headlights swept the strip and the farmhouse. Durell thought he heard the sound of frustrated gunfire, but he couldn't be sure. Turning, he saw that Shan was holding Jasmine in his arms.

He went up forward to sit with the Chinese pilot.

Nineteen

THE MILITARY AIRFIELD NEAR TAIPEI, ON TAIWAN, was the same that Durell had left, weeks before, for the flight to China. The evening air felt lush and tropical, after Peking's autumnal weather. They were met by three husky, polite young men in dark suits straight from Madison Avenue. Identity cards were flashed, indicating they were from K Section, but Durell did not recognize them. It did not necessarily mean anything.

"Our car is over there," the spokesman said. "I'm Fred Ford." He urged them across the warm, dusky field and looked curiously at Durell. "Which one of you is the real Shan?"

Durell ignored the question. "Did McFee send you?"

"Sure." Ford had a quick, easy grin. "Give your weapons to Joe, please."

"And if we don't?"

"This is a military airbase, sir. We have a dozen people spotted here. Would you care to try anything?"

"Are we under arrest?" Durell asked coldly.

"Just normal precautions, sir."

Shan said, "You act as if we were plague bacilli out of China. We're tired, we've just completed a mission——"

"Are *you* Durell? Or are you Shan?"

Shan smiled. "Five gets you one if you spot us."

"He's the Cajun," said the man named Joe. "Durell was always a gambler."

Ford looked annoyed under his polite façade. "All right. Do you give up your weapons or not?"

Durell handed over his gun and knife, and Shan and Jasmine followed. Jasmine said, "I don't believe General McFee sent you. You're either from Haystead's E Branch or Lotus; but not from McFee."

"It doesn't matter, Miss Jones. Come with us."

They were spirited away into a big black car with swift, smooth precision. Another black sedan swung after them as the driver hit the highway into Taipei. Although the air was warm, the windows were kept shut, and the air-conditioning was not used. Durell and Shan were divided by the man named Joe; Jasmine was assigned to the jump seat. Her knees pressed into Shan's thigh, and they looked at each other with silent intimacy. Durell felt a sense of loss as he watched them, and he said to Shan quietly, "Do you recognize any of these men?"

Shan replied in Mandarin. "They were the people who

fished me out of the river and dropped me near Peking to find you."

Joe grinned. "So you're Shan?"

"Perhaps. Perhaps not. We have learned to change places. Durell is Shan; Shan is Durell."

"No need to get snotty about it," Joe grumbled. "We're all on the same side."

"Are we?" Durell asked.

Traffic in Taipei was its usual jumble of rush-hour congestion. Joe kept his gun on his knees between them. They had to stop twice for tangles of carts and buses near the gardens on Yuan Hill, outside the main city. Finally they swung into Chungking North Road, passed a movie house and swarms of pedicabs, and heard the clamorous, uninhibited uproar of a free city. They turned into a palm-lined boulevard leading to Chungshan bridge, heading for Durell's former hotel, the Ma Tsu. Durell asked about it, and Joe said, "Yes, the Sea Goddess Hotel. Your old suite has been kept there for you."

"I have to report to Haystead," Durell said.

"Later, sir."

"I have my orders. If you interfere——"

"I'm sorry. We have orders, too. You have to have a complete debriefing first."

"By whom?"

"We can't say yet. You'll know at the Ma Tsu."

"Then we *are* in custody?" Shan asked.

"You said it, not I."

Nothing was according to the book, Durell thought. Uneasiness grew in him like a dark storm. He did not know these men. They were obviously Americans, from a security agency, but there were always these wheels within wheels, lack of coordination and senseless rivalry between one apparatus and another. He did not think they were from K Section, as they claimed. The Lotus plane that had returned them came from Zebra project, which was under Haystead's E Branch. Haystead had shown no love for McFee. It was as if part of the storm surrounding Durell was meant to strike at K Section and destroy it. He thought about this, and suddenly felt as if he'd caught a loose thread in the knots he had been trying to untangle. He looked at Shan as the car slowed in the traffic near the Chungshan bridge, and an unspoken agreement was made between them in that one look.

He felt as if a crisis were at hand. Either he lived, with Shan, or they would both be dead soon. Shan had put it correctly. There were elements in the intelligence community who regarded them as plague germs, freshly out of mainland China. These elements, suspicious and mistrustful, would sooner silence them than risk the danger of letting them continue.

The big car was halted by a pedicab accident that tangled up traffic near the bridge access. The second car that trailed them was separated by hooting, jingling buses and bicycles.

"Shan?" he said quietly.

Shan nodded. The man named Joe who sat between them was good, but not good enough. Durell chopped at his gun, while Shan slashed at Joe's throat with the edge of his palm. Joe grunted and drew in a long, strangled breath, then bent forward with blood and spittle in his mouth. Durell grabbed the gun. At the same moment, the two in front started to turn in alarm. They were much too late. They were almost amateurs, Durell thought.

"Freeze," he said. "Hands off the wheel, Ford. Foot on the brake. Unlock the doors." He had noted that the rear doors had no handles. "Now!" he said sharply, as Ford hesitated.

"Listen, Shan—or Durell—whichever you are——"

"Shut up."

Shan reached forward carefully and took their weapons and retrieved their own. There were impatient horns and bicycle bells jingling all around them on the bridge approach. The botanical gardens stretched in dusky, tropical green to the right. The pedicab that had been struck by a bus was straightened up now, but there was a distant sound of ambulance sirens hooting across the bridge. All to the good, Durell thought grimly.

"Jasmine?" She hadn't moved on the jump seat. "We'll soon know if these men work for McFee. Come with us."

The driver, with Durell's gun in the nape of his neck, unlocked the car doors. Shan and Jasmine got out. Durell followed routine procedure in backing out of the sedan. He saw men running through the stalled traffic from the car that had followed them in the rear and decided not to waste any more time.

"Let's go."

They ran through the traffic for the park, dodging pedestrians and gaining the paths between tall oleanders and palms. Dusk had fallen, but the street lamps weren't on yet. Durell caught Jasmine's hand and pulled her along. Several times he looked back and thought he saw the men in the dark gray suits running after them, shouting. Then they went out of sight. He turned right, ducked around a bandstand pavilion, turned left, saw the glimmer of Chinese characters in a neon sign, and headed that way. In a few moments they were in a swarm of pedestrian traffic, having circled back to cross the Chungshan bridge. The traffic jam had eased, although the whirling lights of the ambulance still shone behind them.

Shan slowed to a walk. "I am sorry. My injuries——"

"We're all right now," Durell said.

In minutes they were lost in the small, tangled streets across the bridge. A restaurant advertising Cantonese cooking shone lights at them from a narrow alley. They luckily found a table in the crowded place, and Durell took a seat from which he could watch the entrance.

Jasmine looked exhausted. "I don't understand. Are we just going to let them hunt us? I thought we'd be safe when we got here, and all we had to do was report to McFee and Haystead."

"The job isn't done," Durell said grimly. "Unless we find some answers, they'll never let us live."

"But who are 'they'?" she demanded.

"I wish I knew. How do I reach McFee, Jasmine?"

She hesitated, then said, "I have a telephone number. It was to be used when I got back, but only if——" She paused and looked at his duplicate, Shan. "Only if I had to warn McFee."

"Warn him of what?"

"If I—if I thought you were convinced he was the traitor, the top man in the Sentinels."

"Do you think I believe that?"

"I—I don't know."

"Give me the number, Jasmine."

When she told it to him, he asked the harassed Chinese restaurant proprietor for the phone, borrowed some coins from the man, and called the number. The phone rang five or six times. He looked across the crowded restaurant and saw Jasmine talking rapidly and earnestly to Shan. He wished he knew what she was saying. A sense of desperate urgency filled him as the phone went unanswered. He was about to hang up when it clicked.

"Give me McFee," he said. "This is Durell."

He recognized the little man's voice. "Welcome back to never-never land, Cajun."

"It's no time for jokes, General. I'm hot."

"Of course."

"I mean three men saying they were from your office, from K Section, were taking Shan and Jasmine and me for a ride."

"Yes, I understand."

"You don't seem bothered by it, sir."

"I assume you can take care of yourself, Samuel."

"I need help, sir."

"Where did these men say they were taking you?"

"To the Ma Tsu Hotel, where I was before."

"Then go there," McFee said crisply. "That's all I can suggest."

"Listen, is Dierdre still——?"

The telephone clicked and went dead.

Shan asked quietly, "Do you often put your head in the tiger's mouth like this, Cajun?"

"Sometimes it's the only way to see if he means to bite your head off."

"I fear we are surrounded by tigers now."

It was half an hour later, and the Sea Goddess Hotel was crowded with military uniforms and tourists jamming the bar for cocktails. Quite a few disapproving glances met them because of their disheveled clothing. Jasmine offered to get the key from the clerk's desk, and Durell and Shan, aware of the startled looks greeting their identical appearance, waited outside the lobby. The doorman started to ask their business, then saw something in Durell's eyes that made him wander off, excusing himself. A group of high-ranking Air Force officers got out of taxicabs, talking too loudly. One was drunk and was supported by two laughing colonels. There was no sign of the Madison Avenue types who had tried to snatch them at the airport.

Shan said, "She should have had the key by now."

"You seem to worry about Jasmine, Shan."

"Yes, I do."

"Are you fond of her?"

"More than a little, Cajun."

"She's a fine girl," Durell said.

"I am aware of her qualities. I am aware of her love for you. Perhaps there will come a time when she realizes——"

Durell interrupted. "She's been gone too long."

His uneasiness suddenly exploded into a raging alarm. Turning, he threw aside caution and stalked through the crowded, elegant lobby and made for the wing beside the swimming pool. There were colored spotlights under the palms and oleanders, and more lights on the pool and its central statue of Ma Tsu. A few people still lingered over drinks at the poolside tables. Beyond, the path curved through shrubbery to the modern wing he had occupied before. He paid no attention to the curious glances he got as he strode along with Shan, his duplicate, at his heels.

The explosion seemed like the end of the world.

The shock wave and blast hit him in the chest just as he started to mount the outside stairs to the balcony of his former rooms. He staggered, felt as if he had been slammed with the flat of a board, and stumbled back against Shan. The rumbling echoes of the explosion still rolled over the extravagant hotel gardens when he cursed, heard Shan groan, and then took the steps three and four at a time to reach the room assigned to him.

The door hung crazily on torn hinges. Smoke and acrid fumes still boiled from the shattered rooms within. He heard distant screaming, and then it was as if his senses refused to accept what he saw, and he moved through a cotton-wool fog.

"Jasmine?" Shan murmured. He sounded agonized. He had a cut on his cheek. "She went ahead——"

"It was a booby trap—meant for me. Or for you. It makes no difference." Durell could not recognize the sound of his own voice. "Stay here, Shan."

"No, I go in with you." His voice was harsh. "McFee arranged this. He fears you and what you may have learned."

"Shut up," Durell said fiercely.

He walked through the shattered living room and into the bedroom of the suite. He saw blood on the wall, and more blood on the floor, and a piece of Jasmine's blue cotton suit. It was as if everything stopped inside him.

She lay near the foot of the bed, and for a moment he thought she had escaped miraculously. Her face was untouched. Her eyes were open, and he thought she was watching him as he entered, for she had a small, pleased smile on her face, as if she had accomplished something she had always longed for.

But Jasmine was dead.

Twenty

HALF AN HOUR LATER, HE WALKED SILENTLY WITH Shan through the crowded streets of downtown Taipei. He had reacted automatically, pushing Shan outside, although the Chinese had wanted to linger beside the dead girl. In the confusion that filled the hotel after the bomb blast, it had been simple to slip away, although Durell was sure that a report of the "twin Chinese" would inevitably reach intelligence headquarters. He had no illusions about his capacity to stay free for very long. Against the massed and organized forces opposing him, the state efficiency of the Kuomintang would soon stop him. He had no illusions, either, as to what would happen if he were caught. He would not be held for questioning. The word was out to shoot to kill, instantly.

For the moment, they were reasonably safe in the crowded streets, the lighted shops and restaurants. Shan shared his silence for long minutes. Then he said, as if he had been considering it for some time, "The bomb was meant for us. For you. McFee ordered you to the Ma Tsu. So he wants you dead."

"If so, he killed Jasmine," Durell said grimly.

"You cared much for her?"

"Yes. Much."

"And I, too," Shan confessed. "Like a flower that was suddenly watered and blossomed. As if I had come out of a wide and hostile desert. We—we understood each other."

"I know."

"I've been with L-5 for many years, as you have been with K Section," said Shan. "We are not only alike in looks, for the present, but similar inside, adjusted to our world. There is no place for emotion in it. You and I have both lost good friends in years past; we accept it and try to forget and never seek useless vengeance. To allow private emotion to distract us is a certain way to quick death for ourselves. And yet——"

"What are you trying to say?" Durell asked.

"I have lost everything. I need not keep to the rules that have kept me alive all these years."

"Meaning?"

Shan said, "I am going to kill your Dickinson McFee. You can do it, if you wish; if you do not, then I shall."

"Because of Jasmine?"

"And other reasons."

"I think it's time you gave them to me," Durell said.

It felt strange to accept this Chinese as an ally when he normally would have been a deadly enemy. But he broke all rules of logic and trusted Shan. He expected Shan's decision to kill McFee. Evidence had piled up, one straw after the other, to form a damning pattern. He felt as if he had been thrust outside of his old loyalty to K Section. He had been betrayed and had escaped death several times by narrow margins. He could not deny his bitterness and resentment, and he did not like to think of himself as a pawn in a game that might destroy the world.

"Name the other reasons, Shan," he insisted.

They paused at a traffic light, crossed with a surge of chattering Taiwanese, and entered an arcade filled with bright neon Chinese characters. No one had followed them, for the moment.

"It is true," Shan said slowly, "I have not told you all I know. My job was to learn about the Six Sentinels. What happened to Jasmine confirms all I suspected. Only McFee, and his men who picked us up at the airfield, knew we were going to the Sea Goddess Hotel."

"*If* those were McFee's men. They could have been working for Haystead. He should be checked out first."

"Haystead's office in the I.P.S. building is impregnable. That was how I happened to be caught the first time, remember?" Shan paused. "It was McFee who sent Chien Y-Wu into China as a false defector. McFee ordered Chien to enrage the Chinese regime and incite them into a nuclear attack on Taiwan and the renegade Nationalists." Shan smiled thinly. "I think I know more about your boss than you do. We have good people in Washington. Did you know that McFee is heavily in debt, to the tune, as you say, of over two hundred thousand dollars?"

"I don't believe it," Durell said flatly.

"What do you know of his private life?"

"Very little," Durell admitted, "but——"

"Unfortunately, I can prove almost nothing to you. But he is heavily in debt to Senator Haystead—the General's uncle, the far-right reactionary in your government who has been the seat and center of a number of conservative plots and cabals."

"Why did McFee borrow that much money? And why from a man like Senator Haystead?"

"I cannot say. I do not know."

"You'll have to prove all this to me," Durell demanded.

"I can prove only part of it." Shan's eyes were opaque. "I worked on the Six Sentinels job for many months. I am not inefficient. I know my job." He hesitated again. "I can give you half the names of the six military and political men who comprise the cabal known as the Six Sentinels."

Durell sighed softly. "Half is better than none."

"Only half of each. None is complete. It is a code list that Colonel Chu had, and which I stole from him. It was one reason he was so anxious to see me dead. And the list is all in symbols. I have never learned the key to the other half. It is like a piece of torn currency, you see. Without the other half to match it, the list will buy you nothing."

"Do you have it with you?"

Shan tapped his forehead. "It is in my mind. Dragon, White Horse, Yellow Tiger, Blossom of Tranquillity, Pink Cloud, and Far Mountain."

Durell stared at him. "What does all that mean?"

"Those are the Six Sentinels."

"They have no value as they are," Durell objected.

"You have them fixed in your mind? Well, then, McFee has the other half, the key, so to speak, that will translate those names into the names of well-known, powerful personages in the United States."

Durell sighed. "Not good enough."

"Then get the rest from McFee," Shan suggested. "If you do not, I shall. You have until morning. After that, I will do what I must." He made the slightest movement of his hand in his pocket. "No, do not try to stop me or keep me with you, Cajun. We have been allies until now. But since Jasmine's death—well, I must do as my conscience dictates and kill McFee if you do not."

"McFee is a clever and dangerous man."

"I can do it," said Shan. "So can you. It is McFee's life, or ours."

"You sound sure of yourself."

They stared at each other in the garishly lighted arcade. Over Shan's shoulder, Durell saw a blue-uniformed policeman pause and scan the crowd of teen-age Chinese inside. He turned his back and walked with Shan toward the rear entrance, which debouched on the next narrow street. The evening air was filled with the smells of cooking and wine and the inescapable effluvium that marks every Oriental city. Shan touched his shoulder. "I will find you at dawn. Do not try to stop me. When we meet again, you can report what you have done. After that, our alliance may come to an end."

Durell did not try to stop him.

He moved like a lonely shadow through the darkening streets of Taipei. He had kept the Chinese automatic machine-pistol, and its weight was comforting in his coat. Durell was accustomed to working alone and felt a sense of freedom as he proceeded. He knew what had to be done. Everything that had gone before had been a series of tricks like those on a magician's stage. He saw his way clearly now. When the image of Jasmine's death crossed his mind, he drew a curtain over it.

He decided to hit General Harry Haystead first.

I.P.S. Electronics, E Branch headquarters, was surrounded by a high fence topped by wire, electronic sensors of infrared and body-heat detection, sound devices, and explosives. It stood in stark modernity amid Taipei's small, tangled streets. Floodlights made the gate impossible. The windows of the office where he had been briefed by the bluff, fanatic Air Force general were brightly lighted. He made a wide circuit of the building, noted cars parked in the guarded lot, saw the brief shadow of a dog race across the open area, as if pacing him, and then retired. He knew better than to try to force his way in.

From a nearby telephone booth, he dialed Haystead's number. The operator gave him a tired secretary with a Bronx accent, and she told him Haystead was in conference.

"Tell him it's Durell," he said shortly.

"Who?"

"Or Major Shan."

"Oh. Justa minnit."

It took ten seconds. Haystead was cordial. "Cajun? For God's sake, I've been waiting—where are you?"

"Don't tap the line. I won't be here for more than a few minutes. I don't trust you."

"Look, I heard about that poor girl. I swear to God we didn't have anything to do with it!"

"You son of a bitch," Durell said.

"What?"

"You set me up from the start."

"No, I tell you, it was an open assignment. You were to shut Chien's mouth in Peking——"

"It's shut. He's dead, you bastard."

There was silence, punctuated only by Haystead's hard breathing. "Look here, I'm not accustomed to being addressed——"

"Come out of that fort of yours and talk to me."

"Impossible. There's a conference going on. I give you my word, you'll be safe here. Safer than on the streets, or wherever you are. I urge you to come in for sanctuary."

"Against whom?"

"You got a lot of people sore at you, Cajun."

"What did I do wrong?"

"Nothing. You did all the right things. So they'll kill you. They think you know too much."

"About the Six Sentinels?"

"That's right, Cajun." The man's voice went hoarse. "Look here, it's imperative that you report to me at once. Otherwise, it's all wasted, you understand? You're a dead man if you don't take sanctuary."

"Come and meet me," Durell said.

"No, I can't——"

"On my terms. My time and place."

"I don't trust you, Cajun."

"That makes it mutual," Durell said and hung up.

He felt dissatisfied. Haystead seemed genuinely desperate to help. It might be the truth; it might not. He felt as if he were on a toboggan ride, slamming downhill at a breakneck speed, with no one to steer him. He had never felt so alone. He walked quickly away from the telephone, found a crowded food stand a block down the street, ordered a bowl of noodles, and waited and watched. Haystead's men came on fast. Two cars blocked off the arcade and uniformed policemen tumbled out, cordoning off the area. Durell watched from a distance. He did not spot any of the gray-suited hoods who had met him at the airfield. When he had seen enough, he faded away.

McFee was next.

He found his way to the old temple lodgings that McFee had used as his own headquarters for K Section's Control in Taipei. It was after ten o'clock at night. The thought of Jasmine's death began to ride him like a waking nightmare, and now he could not shake it off.

In contrast to Haystead's headquarters, everything about K Section's Control was dark, shut up tight, and looked abandoned. He did not believe it. The low Chinese building brooded before him like a trap waiting to be sprung. He told himself to quit, that he was not thinking clearly, but he had come a long way since his strange, hostile interview with McFee over two weeks ago. McFee had sent him into China almost certain that he would never return. McFee knew he was back now, certainly. Durell had known tough opponents in the past, but McFee would be the toughest. He didn't doubt now that McFee had the answers he needed in order to survive. He was certain of this as he had never been certain of anything before.

Every step of the way, he thought, he had been confronted by evidence pointing to McFee who, for reasons of his own, had been ready to sacrifice him and destroy the troubleshooting K Section branch of the C.I.A. Two weeks ago, he would have scorned the thought. He had worked too long for the general to take such a premise lightly. He knew he had been groomed by Haystead, who was convinced of McFee's guilt in the Six Sentinels conspiracy. Everything that had happened was just frosting on the cake. Haystead had prepared him to kill McFee.

And now, since Jasmine's death, he was almost convinced that Haystead was right.

At the same time, he felt oddly detached from the problem. Perhaps he had been carefully fashioned as a lethal instrument to remove McFee, and except for this thought, his mind felt blurry about all that had happened. It was almost as if some dark drug had been injected in him, turning him into a hunting predator with only a single-minded objective.

If McFee was dangerous, so was he. Durell was aware of his own capacities. He could kill, if necessary, in a dozen swift and efficient ways. He did not enjoy it, but when it had to be done, he did it, and put the event quickly from his mind afterward. It was one reason his dossier at L-5 in Peking and at the former KGB headquarters in Moscow—now reverted to the MVD—Ministerstsvo Vnutrennikh Dyel—was marked with the red tab indicating: DANGEROUS—KILL ON SIGHT.

Still, McFee had taught him most of the tricks of this deadly game, and he moved with utmost caution.

The nearby Buddhist temple, adjacent to the long, low building where he had first met McFee in Taipei, was fully lit, with saffron-robed priests moving about and sounding gongs in some sort of ceremony. A low compound wall separated K Section's Control from the brightly lighted temple. He walked by it, mingling with the crowd of Chinese about the entrance. There was a separate moon gate around the corner that yielded into a path across a garden to the main house door. Durell watched it for twenty minutes, saw no one, spotted no movement through the circular entrance. There were carved stone good-luck tiger dogs on either side of the gate, and from his vantage point he saw a lighted stone lantern in the garden. But all the windows remained dark.

He had no doubt that somewhere inside, McFee was waiting for him.

At last he spotted a low-growing banyan tree whose roots and branches could get him over the wall. He moved at once from the shadows of the doorway where he had stood and followed a small group of Chinese, led by a saffron-robed priest. No one paid any attention to him. The sound of gongs and chanting filled the street. He looked as Chinese as the others around him, and he reminded himself that he could fade away anonymously if necessary.

When he passed the banyan tree, he dropped back and flattened against its wide, rooty bole. The shadows were friendly. With the procession safely past, he jumped, then climbed up the numerous hanging roots that descended into the rough ground. He took his time. Every grip, every branch had to be studied with care before he moved on. At last he was level with the top of the compound wall. The light available was only a dim reflection from the temple area nearby, but he managed to trace the fine, delicate wires that had been laid on top of the stone wall. It would be lethal to touch them, he decided.

He climbed to a higher branch, placing his hands and feet carefully. The faintest humming touched his ear, and he froze. The noise, no louder than the drone of an insect, was momentarily drowned by the cymbals from the temple. Then he heard it again. He scanned the leafy branches around him. With one long leap, he could make it down over the wall and inside the garden. That, too, could be deadly. He did nothing for five minutes while he searched among the leaves. Then he spotted a faint metallic reflection behind a twig, carefully reached up, and exposed a tiny microphone wired there. It would be powerful enough to pick up his breathing, he thought grimly. And if there was one device, there would be others. Perhaps he had been detected already.

He decided to retreat.

With the first move, he sprang a defense trap. His foot came down on a small twig sprouting from the lower branch. There was a click and a snap and he let go of everything and let himself drop. A branch came up like the lash of a whip and he felt something slash across his forearm. He glimpsed the bright sheen of a razor-sharp knife flashing past his eyes, and he fell, stunned and in pain.

He landed backward, flattening his hands behind him, rolled over across the uneven sidewalk, and came up fast.

Nothing else happened. There was a rustling in the dark branches of the banyan tree above, and that was all. His arm burned and pained him, and he rolled back his coat sleeve to look at the long rip in his forearm. Blood flowed from the wound. He wondered briefly if the knife-point in the booby trap had been touched with poison; but there was no use worrying about that. He tore his shirt with his teeth, made a temporary bandage about the wound, and sat down again to catch his breath, leaning against the compound wall.

There were no other alarms. Inside the dark house he knew there would be an indicator panel showing that this deadly little device had gone off. Someone would come to investigate, but they would take their time and be careful.

The place was impregnable, he decided. Knowing McFee, he guessed that this knife trap was only one of dozens waiting for an unwelcome intruder.

He couldn't reach McFee this way.

There was only one other way he could do it.

Twenty-one

DURELL HAD KNOWN DEIRDRE PADGETT ALMOST from his first assignment with K Section. Through the years as a field officer, he had heard Deirdre declare her love in a hundred different ways. There was a time when he had considered marriage, and then dismissed it as impractical, as making him vulnerable in this business. He had not been able to bring himself to leave K Section when he could still live a normal life; and then it had been too late. He had known many women, but Deirdre, with her silken black hair and blue eyes, was special, something private and wonderful and beautiful in his otherwise grim and dangerous life. Eventually, Deirdre had taken a job with K Section, too, against all his arguments, and Dickinson McFee had made her a special assistant.

She had been here in Taipei when he left for mainland China, and if McFee were still here, she could be found, too.

He had never imagined using her for his own purposes before; but then, he thought, he had never been in such a desperate situation before.

She could be the key to unlocking McFee's defenses.

Dr. Ike Greentree came awake with a start, one arm flailing across his face in the darkness. Durell caught his wrist and pinned it to the pillow and sat on the edge of the bed.

"Keep quiet, Ike. It's all right."

"What? What?"

"I'm Sam. Cajun. Take it easy."

It was past midnight, and Durell had walked halfway across the city, keeping to dark, lonely alleys, to find the little bungalow where Greentree lived while attached to Haystead's E Branch in Taipei. He had been in luck to find the surgeon here, instead of at the Sun Moon cottage where the original plastic surgery had been performed. The bungalow, deep in the shadows of tropical shrubbery on a quiet street, had proved to be without gimmicks or alarms.

"Wait—wait a minute," Greentree said fuzzily.

"Take your time. Take ten seconds."

"Can I put on a light?"

"I'll do it."

There was a small bedside lamp, and Durell made sure the draperies were drawn securely before he put it on. Greentree blinked and grunted in the glare, and turned on one hip amid the tangled sheets to grope for his glasses. Durell handed them to him, and Greentree sat up, wiped a shaking hand across his mouth, and stared at him.

He asked at once, "Which Shan are you?"

"I'm Durell. Did you know the real Shan is alive?"

"I heard about it a few days ago."

"McFee told you?"

"Right. Glad you're back safely, Cajun. Really glad. The job I did looks good, eh? It took you to Peking and back."

"You did a fine job, Ike."

"Everything okay, then?"

"You know damned well it isn't," said Durell.

Greentree looked about the bedroom as if searching for something. His eyes behind his glasses slowly assumed the cool intellectuality that was usual with him. His hands stopped shaking.

"You scared hell out of me, Cajun."

"Why?"

"Well, you know—midnight awakening—intruder in the place——" Greentree started to get out of bed, and Durell eased him firmly back with a hand on his chest. "I'm not accustomed to your cloak-and-dagger methods, that sort of thing. I'm a surgeon, not a field agent, like you."

"And you know I'm *persona non grata*, is that it?"

"Have you reported to Haystead yet? Or to McFee?"

"You mean, have I stretched my throat for the butcher's knife? Not yet, Ike. I don't intend to."

"Now, look, I'm only part of the job in doing the plastic surgery on you and changing you back. That's all I know."

"Good. We'll keep it that way. But there's one thing I want from you, Ike, and I want it fast and honest. I have to find Deirdre, and I need her now."

"Your girl? But that doesn't make sense——"

"Ike, I happen to know you have an I.Q. of 148 and a reputation for being a very cool customer. Don't play games with me. Tell me where to find Deirdre, and don't lie. You know where she lives in Taipei. She wouldn't be away from McFee during business hours, but McFee would set her up with living quarters out of that fort he has across town. So tell me where she lives. You've been there for cocktails more than once, haven't you?" Durell guessed.

"Well, yes, but——"

"Give me her address."

"You sound off your rocker, Cajun. That may not be a very professional description, but I think you're suffering from exhaustion, an induced form of suppressed hysteria, fatigue——"

"Shut up, Ike. I want to find Deirdre."

"What for? I don't care to be involved——"

"You won't be. If you don't talk, I'll have to hurt you a bit, Ike. I don't want to do that."

"You wouldn't——" The surgeon paused and stared at Durell for a calculating moment. What he saw in Durell's face and eyes decided him. "Yes, I think you would. I thought we were friends."

"No man has friends in this business. Give, Ike."

Greentree muttered the address reluctantly. It was in a nearby residential quarter, a bungalow development similar to his own, almost entirely reserved for American personnel assigned to the Kuomintang government as liaison officers.

"Listen, Cajun, in your present state of mind—you wouldn't hurt her? I heard she's your girl."

"She is. Thanks, Ike. I'm sorry, but I'm going to have to tie you up and tape your mouth, to keep you off the phone for a while. I'll apologize if I make it through this thing."

"I think you're out of your head, Cajun."

"Maybe I am. Get out of bed now."

"What's the matter with your arm? You've been cut——"

"Never mind the professional interest. Let's have some surgical tape from your kit. For your mouth, not my arm."

Deirdre awoke more smoothly than Ike Greentree. Durell found two alarm systems around her bungalow, one a trip wire that he climbed over in the darkness, the other a monitor mike at the bedroom window. His arm began to throb from the knife wound of McFee's booby trap, but he paid no attention to it. It was after one o'clock in the morning now. Darkness was his ally. At dawn's light he would be a sitting duck for every counterintelligence apparatus on Taiwan. He thought wryly that matters had been simpler and more clearly defined in the heart of Peking.

It took ten minutes to jump the window bug, tracing the delicate wires to avoid alarm. He didn't doubt that the system ran straight to wherever McFee was waiting for him. But his entry into Deirdre Padgett's bedroom was as soundless as the movement of a dark shadow.

He stood over her bed for a quiet moment. A trace of silver moonlight touched her long, black hair spread over the white pillow. In her sleep, her face was a lovely oval, intimately familiar, dearly beloved; it showed her usual serenity, but she also frowned slightly, as if she were having a bad dream. He touched her bare shoulder lightly, bent and kissed her. In the moonlight the dark fans of her lashes lifted and fluttered, then her blue eyes were wide, looking up at him. Her mouth opened, and her lips trembled for a moment.

"Sam?" she whispered.

"Right," he said quietly. "Don't shout, don't cry out, don't raise an alarm."

"Why should I?" she asked.

He towered over her bed. She had made no effort to sit up. His Chinese face was immobile, implacable. "Why didn't you stay with McFee tonight?"

"He sent me home."

He felt danger. "To wait for me?"

"He didn't think you'd find me. Are you all right, Sam? You look—it must have been difficult."

"Yes, it was."

"What's the matter with your arm?"

"Never mind. Get up and get dressed, Dee."

"You sound strange."

"I feel strange. Get up."

She tried to smile. "Is that an order?"

"Yes."

"Sam, darling, let's not quarrel. I was foolish to be jealous of your going off with Jasmine."

"You don't have to worry about Jasmine any more. She's dead. She took a booby-trap bomb that was meant for me."

She was inexpressibly shocked. "Jasmine——?"

"Yes, that's right."

"You talk about it as if it were just—just a change in the weather."

"It is, in a way. Get up," he said a third time.

"Sam, we've known each other—we've loved each other too long for you to talk to me like this."

"I'm sorry. I'm in the worst trouble of my life, and I need your help."

"Of course I'll help you."

"I have to get to McFee."

"But what's to stop you?"

"If he doesn't have the right answers," he said quietly, "I may have to kill him."

She had started out of bed, moving her long legs over the edge. She had a full, high-breasted body that the moonlight amply outlined. He was suddenly flooded with past intimacies of many close and tender days and nights he had spent with her. She knew him better, perhaps, than anyone else in the world. But now she stared at him with the cold eyes of a stranger.

"You don't mean that," she whispered.

"I do."

"So they got to you, after all?"

"Who are 'they'?"

"I don't know. You have more facts than I."

"I know only half-truths." He quoted the partial list of Sentinel code names to her. " 'Dragon, White Horse, Yellow Tiger, Blossom of Tranquillity, Pink Cloud, Far Mountain.' What do they mean, Dee?"

Her face froze. "Where did you get that?"

"Never mind. What's the other half of those names?"

"I don't know."

"Did you ever hear them before?"

"No, Sam."

"You never lied to me in the past," he said harshly.

"I'm not lying to you now."

"But they mean something to you!"

She was silent, then said, "In your present state of mind, Sam, I don't think I can take you to McFee. I can't let you do it. He'll kill you first if he guesses what you have in mind. He means to save K Section. Certain others want to destroy it, and McFee too, because he and K Section stand in their way. He's fighting for his life, just as you are. He'd hoped you would come back with proof of something that might help him, and at the same time, he's concerned with the false evidence that's been arranged around him. He was half certain you would be brainwashed by it. And you have been."

It was his turn to be still. Her voice was cold, the voice of an enemy. He stared at her in disbelief, feeling as if it were the end of his world. He loved her. He had often protcted her from the dangers of his work. He watched her get out of bed, moving with that lithe and supple grace he knew so well. He suddenly ached for her. But he did not move. She looked at the Chinese gun in his hand.

"If I refuse to help you, would you shoot me, Sam?"

"I can make you take me to McFee."

"Yes, you have ways of hurting, of imposing your will on someone's body."

"I'll do it if I have to," he said.

She stood very still, looking at him across the moonlite bedroom. He thought she had never looked so proud and beautiful. He ached with an illness he knew might never be cured. He wished for many things, and most of all he wished he did not have to do this thing. But he knew he had to go ahead with it.

She dressed quietly and quickly, choosing a dark silk skirt, a dark blue blouse. Her brush crackled as she arranged her thick black hair with gestures he knew well. The silence and the distance grew between them, and he knew that soon the gulf he had created might never be bridged again.

She spoke only once more. "Did you love Jasmine so much, Sam?"

"No," he said. "But I won't accept the reason for her death."

Twenty-two

THE NIGHT TURNED COOL. A WIND RUSTLED THE shrubbery and sent a scatter of brightly colored paper down the street. Deidre moved ahead in proud, angry silence. She had a little Japanese Toyota, and he made her park it some distance from K Section's Control. The Buddhist temple was dark now. The priests had ended their chanting, and the cymbals and gongs were silent. Only the sound of the cool wind came down the street.

Deidre led him around a corner from the side where he had tried to enter before. The wall was blank, but she moved with assurance. Walking half a step behind her, he felt a sudden fear lest she might be hurt in a trap she might not know about.

"Wait, Dee."

She halted passively; her eyes scorned him.

"Tell me how to get in," he said.

"I have to do it myself. My configuration—portrait—call it what you wish, will match the scanners and admit me. The scanner is programmed to allow only certain personnel to enter at night without challenge."

"Suppose I went first?"

"There would be an alarm. If you pushed on, there would be weapons. You wouldn't make it, not even you, Sam."

"Yes, I know how clever McFee can be."

She passed the wall and crossed the street to the house on the next corner. It was a small souvenir shop, rather shabby. She went into the recessed doorway and touched an ugly ceramic dog that guarded the portal, turning its head slightly. The door opened silently. Durell could make out only the dim counters and stacked shelves inside.

"I want to go first," he said.

"You'll be killed if you do. Stand close behind me."

She walked straight through the shop to a beaded curtain in the rear, turned left in the darkness, and went down a flight of wooden steps into the cellar. There were cartons of merchandise stored here, visible in the faint glow of a night light. Durell walked close on Deirdre's heels. The scanner might be confused that way, he thought. He hoped so. He listened for an alarm, but he heard nothing.

Behind the crates was a long, dim corridor and a flight of stairs going up, again lighted by a dim bulb. Deirdre walked in resentful silence. At the top of the second flight, she halted before a closed door.

"Sam, it won't work. He's ready for you."

"How do you know?"

"I know Dickinson McFee. Please, go back. Telephone him. Tell him you've thought things over. Tell him you want an explanation, that's all. Don't accuse him, don't threaten him. He's determined to survive."

"So am I," he said grimly. "Go on."

"I—I'm afraid for you," she confessed.

"I wonder. Maybe you're just afraid for McFee."

"Sam, put that gun away. I'm not afraid for myself, you understand. But it's foolish—you're not yourself, you're not thinking clearly, you've changed——"

"Maybe I've really become Shan," he said grimly.

She sighed and pushed open the door.

McFee said: "That is quite far enough. Thank you, Deirdre. Step to one side, my dear."

They had entered a room furnished as an office, the sort that might be found anywhere in a fine building in the States. There was a massive desk, set against gold-curtained windows, several soft armchairs, a Victorian hat rack, straw Taiwanese rugs. McFee sat behind the desk. On the desk were gray metal cabinets, not very large, with rows of telltale lights and buttons on a sloping control board. One of the telltales blinked rapidly. McFee reached out slowly, his eyes on Durell's tall figure, and pushed a button. There was a click, and the light went out.

"Stay where you are, Dee," Durell said. He kept his gun in hand.

She stood still. McFee Looked small and gray and infinitely formidable behind the desk. His face had never seemed more hostile or dangerous, Durell thought— merely because it was so expressionless. His left hand still rested on the control panel; his right hand held his familiar and deadly blackthorn walking stick, which Durell knew was packed with a minute arsenal of deadly weapons. In the tip of it, he knew, were poison darts. And the tip was pointed directly at him.

"Samuel, you were always something of a Don Quixote, tilting at windmills, although you pride yourself on being a pragmatist. Our psychiatric configurations on you confirmed this some time ago. But I am not a windmill, Samuel. If you move to attack me, you will be killed. I promise you this. I do not threaten it. I have been ready for you, as you see. Don't blame Deirdre; she did not betray you. She did as you asked, and I expected you to ask her to bring you to me." McFee's gray eyes flicked to Durell's bandaged arm. "I am glad the knife did not hit anything vital."

Durell believed him. He saw Deirdre draw a deep breath. She stood ahead and a little to the left of him, but she was still between them. It was an impasse. But he was at a disadvantage. McFee knew he would not expose her to danger; and he already had, by forcing her here. At any moment, McFee might press this advantage somehow; and for the first time in his life, Durell was not sure how he would react. He swore silently at himself for thinking he could bluff this through; when he looked at McFee's icy eyes, he knew the little man realized his advantage.

Would he be killed? He saw death in McFee's face, a tiny spasm of anger at—betrayal?

He said quietly, "I've only come for facts, sir. I'm being hunted by people I don't know. Maybe they're from General Haystead, maybe they're from you, but——"

"Those men who saved Shan and who killed Jasmine —however unwittingly—came from neither of us. I have no love for Harry Haystead. He means to destroy me and K Section. But he's only a tool, as you've become a tool, for other forces."

"Explain it," Durell said.

"Would you use your gun on me, Samuel?"

"If I decide you are guilty, yes."

"Guilty of what?"

"High treason. Planning a nuclear preventive war. Behind the head of, or part of, the Six Sentinels."

"You have been convinced by evidence?" McFee asked coldly.

"The odds are that you are guilty."

"I know the odds. I know the appearances. Do you believe them?"

"I believe nothing. I know nothing. That's why I'm here. To ask for answers."

"With your gun in Deirdre's back?"

"I'll use any means necessary."

"Would you truly shoot her? And me?"

Durell saw a slight change in the gray man's face. McFee's eyes flicked past him for a brief instant, then touched Deirdre's still, stiff figure. He smiled slightly. Durell resisted the impulse to turn his head and see what McFee had looked at. The door had been locked behind him, but he had the feeling of eyes fixed on the back of his neck.

"Be at ease, Samuel," McFee said. His voice, as always, held a note of calm, old-fashioned courtesy; he was a man who would never be startled into betraying his composure. "I can imagine the stories you have heard about my debts—which do not exist—and my fanatic decision that the only solution to this dark underground war in which I have been engaged—and you, too—may be a final holocaust to decide which state is to be supreme in the world. You should know me better by now."

"I don't think I know you at all, sir," Durell said.

McFee nodded. "Which is as it should be. Do you think you are alone in walking with danger every moment of your life? I built K Section, I created it, I commanded it from its inception. The work we have done may have been useless, even preposterous, to achieve our purpose. The men who have died on assignments—your friends and mine—may have died for an irony of history that makes their deaths meaningless. But I cannot believe that."

"Neither can I," said Durell.

"Freedom is a word often abused, made use of by friend and foe alike. Today, semantics is a tool for politics. We are afraid to call a spade a spade. We cover up unpleasant things with sweet icings of words. But you and I have risked our lives, and live in momentary threat of death, for a good purpose. Can you believe I would betray myself, and all the men of K Section who have died, by joining such a foul and irresponsible plot as the Six Sentinels?"

Durell gave no answer. McFee sighed and looked at his deadly blackthorn stick.

"Samuel, I can prove nothing. To attempt to prove my innocence to you is like answering the question of when I stopped beating my wife." The gray man's mouth twitched. "You did not know I was married? I have been married for forty-two years. I have grandchildren. They live under another name than mine, to protect them. I rarely see them. I don't dare visit them. You know the reasons for that. They are the same reasons for which you have refused to marry Deirdre all these years."

Deirdre moved slightly, then was motionless again. Durell could see her proud and lovely profile, but he could not take his eyes from McFee. He spoke quietly.

"I understand what I was supposed to do. You lent me to Haystead's E Branch, ostensibly to kill or rescue Chien Y-Wu before he gave the Chinese the details of our Lotus device. The real motive was to let Haystead use me in the hope that I'd learn something to get you off the hook, General. Haystead is out to smash K Section. A question of bureaucratic rivalry, perhaps. It's happened before. The Six Sentinels also want to wipe out K Section. Their reasons may be even more obvious. But I was meant to be made a tool by which you could be destroyed."

"Exactly, Samuel."

"Is Haystead really innocent? Is he a tool, too?"

"Yes," McFee said.

Durell was surprised, but did not show it. "Then who really runs E Branch? The answer seems plain. The Sentinels have infiltrated either E Branch or K Section, and they use either or both outfits to incite and promote nuclear war with Red China."

"Yes," McFee said again.

"Who are they?"

"I do not know."

"No leads at all?"

"Some."

"I have some leads, too," Durell said.

"I had been hoping you would get something."

Durell's gun felt extraordinarily heavy in his hand. He was aware of a dragging fatigue, a sense of disorientation, as he faced Dickinson McFee. He heard Deirdre draw a small breath, but she did not move, as if she feared any interruption on her part that might shatter the delicate balance here, like a crystal. Then she said, "Sam, I beg of you. Listen to McFee."

"He'll still kill me, I think," Durell said.

"Yes, I may," McFee said. "Give me what you learned in China."

"I got it from Shan," Durell said. "I don't know how valid it may be. It's meaningless to me, anyway."

McFee seemed to tighten up behind his desk.

"A code list?"

"Half of one."

"Can you recite it?"

Durell looked at him and suddenly felt as if he had turned a corner. Anger changed in him, now directed against those who had duped him and brought him to this impossible situation where, to survive, he might see Deirdre killed. "The names are Dragon, White Horse, Yellow Tiger, Blossom of Tranquillity, Pink Cloud, Far Mountain."

McFee looked at him and said calmly, "That is all?"

"For whatever it's worth."

McFee said softly, "That's good. Oh, very, very good, Samuel. I knew you would do it."

"Do you know what the names mean?"

"I have the other half of the code. . . . Samuel, where is Shan now?"

"He thinks you are one of the Sentinels. He's given me until dawn, and then he'll kill you himself."

"Other men have tried. Shan is very talented, though." McFee suddenly stood up, hands flat on the desk, and with one finger, pushed his blackthorn stick aside so that it pointed to the wall. "Come with me, Samuel. You, too, Deirdre."

Durell did not move. "Where?"

"To learn the names of the conspirators, of course. That's your job. It is mine, too. If we are lucky, this will be wrapped up in twenty minutes."

They entered the adjacent temple by the back way. Durell had put his gun away, and walked in silence beside Deirdre. McFee led the way, moving with his usual quick, light gait. The night was cool. There was no moon, and the alley was dark. If there had been anyone else in the Control house, Durell had seen no evidence of it. When he spoke of it, McFee shook his head.

"That is not K Section's Center for Taipei. It was used by the Sentinels until two months ago, to forward their plans that used Chien Y-Wu. You stopped that, finally. Before then, I sent two other men, Adams and Vitberg, into China. The Sentinels managed to silence them, then moved out. I moved in. There was no trace of their identities. But the people who picked you up at the airfield were not mine or Haystead's. They were Sentinel men. They don't know it, of course. They think they work for E Branch, in counterintelligence. That does not make them less dangerous, naturally."

The rear gate opened into a narrow walk that crossed a dark, silent garden. A door led them into a dimly lighted back room of the temple. The red glow of a glass lantern made it seem as if they all moved through an infrared film, distorting the statues on the wall shelves. There were tiers of them, each containing a row of Buddhist figures, and a huge brass gong hung from tasseled cords fixed to the red-timbered ceiling. McFee moved silently toward the glimmering, etched brass of the gong.

"Here," he said. "This was used as the key to the code. It's quite new, made to look as if it were an antique. The gong was installed seven months ago, as a charitable gift to the local monks. It was considered the best way to maintain a file of Sentinel personnel."

"A file?" Durell asked.

"An outfit like the Sentinels has an exaggerated idea of the dramatic," McFee said grimly. "Vitberg, who was killed by Black House people when I sent him into China, got a lead on this and managed to transmit it back to me before he was caught by the enemy. But it didn't give me any of the real names."

They paused before the huge brass gong. It was six feet in diameter, and every inch of it was etched with animal figures and Chinese calligraphy. The red lantern did not yield enough light to define the characters clearly. McFee paused and leaned on his stick; Deirdre stood near the door they had used. The temple was silent, and felt empty.

"I've studied this for more hours than I care to admit," McFee said. "But I did not have the key. Let us hope that Shan was not imagining things."

Candles flickered in the main chamber, and Durell went there, to the great smiling, serene statue of Buddha, and took two of the candles and returned to the gong. By the light of the small flames, he began to go over every inch of the great sheet of brass.

"Why do you suppose the Sentinels put everything in the open this way?"

"They could not risk open files," McFee said. "And this was their forward post for action against the mainland. They broke up the key to the code on it and distributed parts to each of the top men. It was a method by which each of them was able to control his fellow conspirators—through fear of revealing the plot to the public."

" 'Dragon,' " Durell said suddenly. "Here it is." His fingers traced the traditional Chinese figure in a central design on the gong. "Can you read Mandarin, General?" Under the etching were tiny Chinese characters. "Man-Beast." He paused. "I make no name out of that, sir." Then he said, "Wait. Man-*Farm,* really."

McFee said, "Manfield. R. D. Manfield. He's a top industrialist in the computer field. Organizer of the U.P.— United Patriots. Manfield personally financed and actually armed members of his crackpot organization until the F.B.I. outlawed them on interstate arms shipments against I.C.C. regulations. Californian. A believer in the occult and manifest destiny."

" 'White Horse,' " Durell read. "Over here. This character could read Pale Mare. Palomar?"

"John Palomar, ex-movie star, silent days, reputed to be a millionaire several times over," McFee said. "Ran for Congress, defeated twice, involved in a gambling syndicate, indicted for malfeasance in office when he was lieutenant-governor of another state. Married five times. His latest bride is seventeen. He's seventy. Another 'Patriot.' "

" 'Yellow Tiger,' " said Durell. "Saffron Cat? No. Gold Cat. The last bit of calligraphy is vague."

McFee's voice tightened. "Feline. James Goldfel. They weren't very clever. He used to own a scandal sheet news syndicate, pandering to sex headlines and perversion. He used to cull crackpot letters to the editors and recruit members to his American Civil Guard units. Paramilitary outfits that attracted neurotics with itchy trigger fingers. The F.B.I. stepped on them, too. But maybe not hard enough."

The last three code names in the center disc of the gong came rapidly, then. "Blossom of Tranquillity" translated into a woman known publicly and simply as "Lily," who had a nationwide column of occult advice, horoscope interpretations, and advice to the lovelorn, although her own marriages and affairs were fables among the Underground sex magazines. "Pink Cloud" was a former Army general known as "Happy" Skyfield, another far-right militant whose speeches and pamphlets were paranoiac diatribes against minorities and anyone who disagreed with his strong-arm theories of civil control. The last, "Far Mountain," was Rocky Westbank, a wealthy yachtsman, international sportsman, member of the jet set and those dim echelons of society that reach public news only through echoes of private brawls, incredibly orgiastic parties, and hints of exotic pleasure cruises that enterprising reporters could only guess at. Westbank had an office building in Hong Kong and was the owner of a string of international hotels scattered all around the world—very private, small, and discreet. The Ma Tsu, the Sea Goddess Hotel in Taipei, was the largest and most obvious of the Westbank hostelries.

There was a long silence after they had decoded the symbols on the gong. McFee nodded to Deirdre, who took a small flash camera from her purse and photographed the brass etchings from several angles. Durell felt as if a vast weight had been lifted from his shoulders. His mind was clear, as if he had awakened from a long, horrifying dream. The temple, however, no longer felt empty and deserted.

McFee said, "I'll get on this list immediately. A cable to Washington will start things rolling—right at the White House. I doubt if we can obtain public indictments of these Sentinels, but the publicity will be enough to create a national outrage and stop them cold. They won't be able to go on with their plans. I believe I owe you thanks, Samuel."

"Not to me. Shan got the key."

"And you got it from Shan." McFee looked exhausted, suddenly. "I think K Section will survive now. It does not matter—it never mattered much—about you and me, Samuel. The Sentinels wielded influence in a hundred directions. Money, social and political and industrial influence gave them their strength. They worked in the dark, and all we need is a ray or two of light to make them shrivel up and wither away. I think the worst is over."

A precise, Oxonian voice spoke behind them.

"Yes, gentlemen. And you are all under arrest."

Durell turned slowly and carefully.

It was Colonel Chu.

The renegade was not alone. Two of the spruce young men who had snatched Durell at the airfield were behind him. They carried automatic weapons at the ready. The colonel was smiling. He looked trim and dapper, his little moustache was neatly groomed, and his black eyes beamed with satisfaction.

"You are surprised, Durell? I arranged for another Lotus plane to transport me. Actually, I had hoped to reach Taipei before you. It was not possible, but the I.P.S. communication system works magnificently. Poor General Haystead! He still thinks he operates E Branch. But his men take orders from me—and I take orders from the Sentinels. I tell you all this because there is no danger you will ever divulge these facts. The code you broke is meaningless, since it dies with you."

McFee said quietly, "Stand aside, Deirdre."

Colonel Chu said, "Remain as you are, young woman. The three of you will die together."

Deirdre did not move. Her blue eyes touched Durell with despair. Chu said, "Durell, drop your gun."

Durell did so. "I'm Shan," he said.

"Really? And where is Durell?"

"Somewhere in Taipei, hunting for you."

"You lie. Shan is dead!"

"You had reports of two of us, identical, in Peking, Chu. Didn't you figure it out? Durell and I met, and we are working together. He will get you. He knows as much as we. McFee sent him."

Chu looked from one to the other. His armed hoodlums wore blank faces. A light bead of perspiration was visible on Chu's young features. He licked his lips. "Yes, yes, there was some confusion in Peking. Reports of two of you, appearing at different places. I placed no credence in it. Even if I did, it could not matter. You—Shan or Durell, whichever you are—and General McFee will be found dead, listed as suicides, and a suitable cover story describing traitorous activities will be circulated in the intelligence community all over the world. Congress will hear of it, and K Section will be abolished. Whatever information you have on the Sentinels will die with you. It is too bad, Shan—or Durell—that you did not believe my arguments in the Black House and kill McFee for me. It seemed logical that you might. A slight miscalculation on my part, but it does not matter now, does it? Please step forward, gentlemen. Away from the gong, please."

No one moved.

Chu said impatiently, "You are foolish if you resist. The girl, you may be sure, will then die most painfully."

"To hell with you," Durell said.

McFee said, "You have no chance, Chu. Your presence here is simply desperate folly. Everything is known, finished. Durell is at the cable office now, wiring Washington the details."

"You lie!"

McFee shrugged. He looked simple and innocuous. "Ask Haystead. He has been informed, too. You and your men will be hunted down by every agency of the government. The Kuomintang on Taiwan will not deal kindly with you, if we don't get you first. You have nowhere to go. The Lotus planes are grounded. We were expecting you, of course. The plane that took you here went with my agreement. You see, we preferred not to leave you in the Black House in Peking, to work against us."

The Chinese flicked his eyes from McFee to Durell's tall figure. He bit his lip, raised his gun impulsively, and Durell's nerves jumped, expecting the same display of temper he had suffered in the Black House cell. At that moment, a shadow moved behind the two men in the temple doorway. He did not hesitate. With one arm, he thrust Deirdre aside, headlong away from the brass gong. With his right elbow, he rammed backward against the sheet of brass, and the clanging, banging echoes filled the little room with deafening resonance. Then he launched himself forward.

Chu's gun crashed, and crashed again. The shadow behind Chu struck forward and became Shan, Durell's duplicate. The two strong-arm men whirled to confront him, and Durell's shoulder hit Chu's stomach, bowled him over, and he felt something slash the side of his face, another blow that deafened his left ear, and then he drove his fist upward, deflecting Chu's stuttering gun. They crashed back against the wall. Chu's body was like a small coil of steel springs. His empty gun smashed repeatedly at Durell's head and shoulders, and he could not hold the Chinese for long. He heard several more shots, and then a sharp pinging noise, and steel glittered in Chu's throat, a long, narrow pin like a dart. The renegade KMT man suddenly stiffened under Durell, his body arched rigidly, his heels drummed the plank floor. Then he suddenly collapsed into a small, limp sack, empty of life.

"That will be quite enough, Samuel. Thank you. And thank you, Shan," said McFee quietly.

General Dickinson McFee wiggled his blackthorn stick. He had fired the poison dart in its tip at Chu's throat. Durell rolled off the Chinese and stood up slowly, looking for Deirdre. She was staring at Shan in amazement. It was the first time she had seen Durell's duplicate. It was Shan who had silenced the other two gunmen with swift efficiency.

"I think," said McFee gently, "that we can clean things up now."

Twenty-three

DURELL LAY IN DARKNESS, THE BANDAGES TIGHT over his eyes, and listened to the sound of a lark in the early dawn outside the bungalow. His face ached—Ike Greentree had tapered off the sedatives. He felt his cheeks and the contours of his jaw with tentative, exploring fingertips. He felt like himself. He was no longer Major Shan of the Black House. He was once again Sam Durell of K Section.

It was ten days later. He had lived in silent solitude except for the plastic surgeon and his Taiwanese nurse, both of whom were more than uncommunicative. Several times he had apologized to Ike for the night he had forced Deirdre's address from him. The last time, Dr. Greentree replied:

"No need to regret it, Sam. McFee warned me to expect you. He thought of everything. He knew you would escape Chu's bullyboys and try for him, then make the effort through me and Deirdre. He's a smart little fellow, that McFee."

Durell thought some unkind thoughts, but did not voice them. He said, "Maybe I'm finished, Ike. Maybe I'll get what Deirdre always wanted—bounced out of K Section."

"Why?"

"Because I was ready to kill McFee."

"He didn't expect anything else. You're not supposed to talk, Sam. Lie still. Stop working your face."

"Where is everybody?"

"Gone."

"Where?"

He could sense Greentree's shrug, although bandages covered his face. "Back to the States. Cleaning up the mess."

"Have you heard anything?"

"I see nothing, hear nothing, say nothing."

"Some monkey."

"That's me," Ike said. "Now shut up."

Durell wondered if Deirdre had gone, too. He did not expect her to forgive him for using her to reach McFee. Even if his move had been anticipated, it didn't make his act less unacceptable. The lark continued to sing in the dawn air over the resort Sun Moon Lake. The wind came through the bungalow windows and smelled of sweet pines. Now and then he thought of Major Shan and wondered what had happened to him. Without Shan's help, he might never have escaped from Peking, might never have helped McFee solve the conspiracy against K Section. He hoped Shan would survive. He rather thought Shan would. But he wished he knew. He felt as if he had been put in isolation these past ten days. He had seen and spoken to no one but Greentree and the somber nurse.

The lark stopped singing as a car came grinding up the steep, pine-clad mountainside from the lakefront. He heard the sound of windbells somewhere. Then Ike Greentree's familiar step returned to the room.

"How do you feel, Sam?"

"Fine."

"Been awake long?"

"Yes."

"Impatient?"

"I have three more days to go, you said."

"There's been an urgent correction. The bandages come off now."

"Who's visiting us?" Durell asked as the car stopped outside the bungalow. "Is it Deirdre? Have you heard from her?"

"Lie still. It won't take a minute. Keep your eyes closed until I tell you to look at your old homely self." Ike laughed. "I wish I knew what the women really saw in you. You looked better when I made you into a Chinese."

"Is everything all right?"

"You're Sam Durell again."

Ten minutes later he opened his eyes to the morning light. He saw nothing at first, and again, as after the first operation, he felt a brief panic that he might be blind. Then shadows formed, blurred and indistinct, and out of them he gradually saw the gold-rimmed spectacles of Ike Greentree, and the surgeon's narrow, intellectual face. Ike was smiling. The room was the same. He was in the big Chinese bed, covered only with a sheet. His face ached. He blinked slowly, once or twice, and felt as if he had the king of all hangovers.

"Your eyes are normal, Sam," Greentree said.

"I'm glad you think so."

"Any pain?"

"Nothing I can't stand."

"A little edema from the scalpel. It's nothing. The puffiness will ease by nightfall. You look fine."

Greentree gave him a mirror. He looked into his familiar face. Yes, he was Sam Durell again. He sighed and rolled over and looked at the window. The light seemed very strong, but he knew he would adjust to it. He sat up. He was naked under the sheets. The wind was scented with pine and flowers. The curtains blew inward. The lark was singing again, and he had never felt more lonely.

"Do I have a visitor?" he asked quietly.

"McFee is here."

"I thought you said he'd gone to the States——"

"He just flew back. Relax, Sam."

"I can't relax."

"Do you want a sedative?"

"No."

"What's the matter with you? I'm not sore at you, Sam," Greentree said. "Nobody is. Here's General McFee."

Greentree vanished quietly as McFee came in. The first thing Durell noted was that the little gray man no longer carried his blackthorn stick. They stared at each other for a long moment, and McFee sat down primly in a finely carved chair and put his hands on his knees, while Durell sat on the edge of the bed and felt estranged. Then Mc-Fee's mouth quirked.

"You are the Cajun again. Greentree is a genius."

"Yes, sir."

"He did a wonderful job, making you look like Shan."

"Yes, sir. What happened to Shan?"

"I offered him a job in Washington. I felt he should not go back to Peking, to his old work in the Black House, against us. At first, Haystead wanted to treat him as a captured spy. It was rather difficult. Haystead is an impetuous man. He was also desperate, as you know. It had been hinted to him, with the same false evidence that had been gathered against me, that his uncle, the senator, was one of the Sentinels. He was much relieved when I told him the name was not on the Sentinel list you helped to decode. He was also happy to root out the traitorous elements that had infiltrated his E Branch."

"Am I still with E Branch, by the way?"

"Haystead discharged you. He feels you were personally disloyal to him." Again McFee's mouth twitched, and Durell realized it was a smile. McFee said, "I've taken you back."

"So what happened to Shan?"

"I helped him to return to China."

Durell relaxed a little. "That's good. You couldn't have trusted him in Washington. He loves China. It's his motherland. I don't blame him. I only hope I never run up against him on another assignment—if I ever get one."

"You have one, Samuel," McFee said. "We're always short of help, you know. I have some tickets here for you, and a briefing sheet. You're going to Venice. It's a simple job. You can consider it an R & R—Rest and Recreation."

"Venice? On the other side of the world?"

"You've been there before," McFee said caustically.

"Yes, sir. I've been in lots of places before, sir. When do I leave for this allegedly restful assignment?"

"Whenever you can. Make it tomorrow."

"Thanks for all the spare time, sir."

"Samuel, I cannot spare you," McFee said gently. "Did you think I could?"

Durell did not look at him. He searched for his clothes, and did not see them. He said casually, "What about the Sentinels?"

"They are being taken care of. It is out of our hands now. The whole story is on a certain White House desk. You can be sure the danger from them is over." McFee paused. "Here are your tickets. Pan Am from Taipei International, to Venice via Washington. There is more material there that I want you to look at for this next piece of work. Take the tickets, Samuel."

There were two of them. Durell lifted his brows. "Are you coming with me, sir?"

"Not just yet."

"Then who——?"

"Deirdre is assigned to the job with you. You will need her. She knows Venice—at least, that part of it you will have to move in—better than you. I think you will find it —ah—interesting."

"But Deirdre hasn't been to see me or even spoken to me——"

"She is here now."

McFee stood up and walked to the door. For the first time, Durell thought the little general looked tired. It was something of a shock to realize that Dickinson McFee was human, too.

He sat alone and waited, listening to the bird calls and watching the morning light filter through the pine trees. It seemed a long time before he heard her footsteps. The car that had brought McFee and Deirdre to the bungalow started up and went away down the mountainside. He wondered if Deirdre had changed her mind and had gone with it. He did not find it in his heart to blame her, if she had. In the past, they had had many differences about his work; she had charged him with valuing it more than their love. Nothing had changed, there. The arguments he had used then were still valid today. He was beyond the ordinary, day-to-day routines that men and women lived by and built their worlds upon. He could never go back to that. He was Sam Durell, of K Section, and would be so until that moment in time, someday, when he slipped and made an error of judgment. There were plenty of enemies still in the world who wanted to see him dead, wanted his file closed permanently. Sooner or later, that day would come. Whatever the efforts of people like McFee, the world was a long way from peace, and peace still remained an illusive dream in the hearts of men. It had always been so, unfortunately. But he lived in daily risk of his life hoping that it need not be so in the future.

He heard the door open, and it seemed as if everything stopped inside him, and then she was there in the morning light, standing very still across the room, looking at him. Her face was quiet, her eyes serene.

"Hello, Sam."

She was beautiful.

He said awkwardly, "I thought for a moment you might have left with McFee."

"I'll never leave you, Sam," she whispered.

Then she came toward him with a brief, impulsive rush that told him all he longed to know.

ENJOY THE OTHER SAM DURELL ADVENTURES

ASSIGNMENT—

ANKARA   R2056   60¢
BLACK VIKING   D1823   50¢
BUDAPEST   R2040   60¢
THE CAIRO DANCERS   D1983   50¢
CARLOTTA CORTEZ   R2088   60¢
CONG HAI KILL   R2011   60¢
THE GIRL IN THE GONDOLA   R2054   60¢
LOWLANDS   R2028   60¢

A Fawcett *Gold Medal Book*

Wherever Paperbacks Are Sold

A Chilling Novel of Intrigue
by the author of the "ASSIGNMENT" series

Edward S. Aarons
GIRL ON THE RUN

Armand O'Bae didn't simply "disappear." He was kidnapped, tortured, and when he refused to talk, what was left of him went hurtling to the ground from an upper-story window. An unfortunate accident, said the gentlemen involved, and more unfortunate that O'Bae had taken with him the sinister secret of a ninth-century treasure—a legendary crypt stuffed to its very limits with gold, and possibly something much more valuable. Something as modern as atomic energy and just as crucial to the nations of Europe.

Now the killers had to get his daughter—the innocent beauty with nowhere to hide, and only one man she could trust. A man from out of her past, who had every reason to hate her . . .

R2142   *A Fawcett Gold Medal Book*   **60¢**

Wherever Paperbacks Are Sold

If your bookdealer is sold out, send cover price plus 10¢ each for postage and handling to Gold Medal Books, Fawcett Publications, Inc., Greenwich, Conn. 06830. If order is for five or more books, there is no postage or handling charge. Order by number and title. No Canadian orders.